The Summer House
in Santorini

Samantha Parks

OneMoreChapter

One More Chapter an imprint of
HarperCollins*Publishers*
The News Building
1 London Bridge Street
London SE1 9GF

www.harpercollins.co.uk

This paperback edition 2019
1

First published in Great Britain in ebook format by
HarperCollins*Publishers* 2019

A catalogue record for this book
is available from the British Library

ISBN: 9780008324452

Set in Birka by Palimpsest Book Production Ltd, Falkirk
Stirlingshire

Printed and bound in Great Britain by
CPI Group (UK) Ltd, Croydon CR0 4YY

MIX
Paper from
responsible sources
FSC™ C007454

To Averi and Shauna, my gorgeous, strong, passionate sisters. When faced with hard decisions, I hope you always choose to stay true to yourselves.

Introduction

Something like four thousand years ago, before Troy had fallen, in the height of the Bronze Age of Greece, a volcano erupted in the Aegean, the force of which is unrivaled to this day. The tiny island of Thera was destroyed, ripped apart from the middle, birthing legends of hidden cities and buried treasure that would perpetuate for millennia to come. The volcano erupted over and over again, its magma chamber refilling and depleting, until the entire area had been devastated beyond recognition.

But Thera did not die. It became Santorini, or Thira, a small archipelago of islands – one large, reverse-C-shaped one and a few smaller ones – with an ecosystem defined by its volcanic history. The ashy soil birthed unbelievable produce, especially grapes for wine. The caldera that had formed from the island's near destruction made for a gorgeous landscape, and tourists eventually found their way to the hidden treasure of Santorini.

In the middle of the island is a small village called *Exo Gonia*, a town where, from some points in the village, the sea can be seen on every side. The roads up into the village are curvy and narrow, lined on both sides by whitewashed walls concealing houses and gardens that extend farther back into the hills than is evident at first glance. At the top of one such road – up the hill from the *Agios Charalambos*, a beautiful yellow church with three crosses atop round spires – is a small white house with three archways out front and views over Kamari and the Aegean Sea.

The house was built with just one bedroom. The four-poster bed was carved by the grandson of the man who built the house. He built the kitchen table as well; a long, trestled work of art with knots in the sides and a shine on the top from so many years of food and wine and love and laughter. And when he was done, he made a new front door from the same wood and hung it proudly in the frame.

The family who lives in this house is a humble one. The man of the house is a builder; his wife, a seamstress. The man has lived in the house his whole life. In fact, the house has been in the man's family for over two hundred years, built by the first of the family to set foot on Santorini, rearing generation after generation of builders who have lovingly cared for and maintained the house, which has remained largely unchanged.

That is, until the man had a son. And that son became a builder, too, and he wanted to add onto the house. But his father wouldn't let him alter it, so he started building in the garden. He had dreams of entertaining guests from all over the world; strangers who would become friends simply by sitting across the knotted table and eating a meal plucked from the garden and sleeping nestled in the hills of the most beautiful island in the world. "The summer house," he called it; the thing that would bring new people and new adventures to their tiny little corner of *Exo Gonia* on the island of Santorini. He decorated it with yellow paint and his hopes of a more exciting life.

Only one person would come to stay in the summer house as long as the man's son lived, but she would change their world forever.

1

Anna had always thought that Manhattan summer was the closest one could get to hell, as least as far as temperature was concerned. But as she stepped off the plane and onto the tarmac in Thira, she realized there was a whole other level to that particular inferno, and it was in Greece. Santorini, to be specific.

The sun shone a blinding white, and Anna scrambled to pull her sunglasses out of her purse. As she put them on and the glare subsided, she saw that the sky was a brilliant blue with not a cloud in sight. Off in the distance to her right, the sky and sea melded together at some point that Anna couldn't quite determine.

The airport itself wasn't much to look at. Anna wasn't sure what she was expecting – a whitewashed stone building with a blue-painted roof and a cross on top, perhaps? – but she was expecting more grandeur than what she saw as she entered the terminal. The building was white, but that was about the only part of it that met her expectations.

Anna was running through in her mind the different ways in which she could introduce herself to her grandparents. "Hi, Mr and Mrs Xenakis. I know we've never met, but I'm your granddaughter, here to sell your summer house out from under you. Hope that's cool."

She'd have to work on that one. Maybe a drink would help.

According to a quick Google search (her international data charges would be through the roof when she got back, but she would manage), the address her sister Lizzy had given her for her grandfather was only about a mile and a half away as the crow flies, but it would take Anna nearly half an hour on a bus to get there, as walking with her three bags was out of the question. So as she went through Immigration – which was incredibly relaxed – she began looking for signs pointing to the buses. Or maybe she'd get to ride a donkey? She remembered seeing in a film once that tourists got to ride donkeys up and down the steep steps, and she started mentally counting her euros to determine if she'd have enough for a donkey ride *and* lunch. How much was a donkey ride, anyway? Five euros? Fifty? She only had fifty with her, so she hoped it was less. Riding a donkey sounded... well, not exactly appealing, but appropriate.

As she walked through Arrivals, she skimmed over some of the signs being held up for people by their drivers, but there was only one sign that made her do a double-take – in big block letters on a piece of cardboard, it said: "LINTON".

The man holding the sign stood out from the others as well, not because he looked familiar, but because he was a head taller than everyone else around him. His thick dark hair fell to just above his shoulders, though the top half was tied back away from his face. His arms were lean but visibly strong, and the contours of his muscular chest were visible through his white tee shirt. He wore khaki pants that were covered in paint. Not your typical car-driver's uniform, but Anna instantly thought of her grandfather's construction company and began to wonder if the man really could be there for her. But no one knew she was coming... did they?

The man waved as Anna walked nearer. So maybe he *was* there for her. Or was he just flirting? If she was being honest, Anna wasn't sure which she preferred.

"You're Anna?" he asked when she was close enough. He knew her name. Damn, not flirting. At least she was getting a ride, though.

"Yeah, that's me," she said, sticking out her hand. The man shook it, his long fingers wrapping firmly around her own, and Anna had to remind herself how a handshake worked. "I didn't realize I was getting picked up."

The man didn't respond; he just tucked the sign under his arm and started walking away, so Anna followed.

"You don't look half-Greek," the man said without turning around.

"Well, I am," Anna said, rolling her eyes. What did it

matter? Half the people in the airport were white and blonde. "Who told you to come pick me up?"

"I work for your grandfather," he said, shoving the sign into a bin as they walked past before carrying on.

Apparently that would have to do for an explanation, as he didn't offer any further insight as to how they knew she was coming. Anna replaced her sunglasses as they went outside, ready for the brightness this time, but the heat still caught her off guard.

"Your English is really good," she said, hobbling behind him as he walked.

"I went to university in London," he replied without turning around.

He kept walking past the cars waiting out front, and Anna figured his car must be in one of the parking areas further on. She struggled to keep up, her duffel bag hitting the backs of her legs, her handbag strap straining against her shoulder and her heels catching on her roller bag as she did a funny little run/walk behind him.

After a couple minutes of walking in silence, him a few paces ahead of her with her legs moving in double-time to keep up, Anna had become confused. They had now walked past the turnoff to the parking areas, assuming a big "P" meant parking in Greece as well. In fact, they were headed out of the airport grounds alto-gether.

"Um, sorry, but where are we going?"

He looked back at her over his shoulder, his eyebrows

pressed together and his mouth in a half-smile, an amused look on his face. "To meet your grandparents, obviously."

"Yeah, but where is your car?"

He laughed. "So sorry, Princess Anna, no car service for you."

Anna frowned, and the man pointed ahead to a bus stop. Dozens of other people were huddled outside.

"I could have taken the bus by myself," she said, hoisting her slipping duffel bag back over her shoulder.

He simply shrugged.

At that moment, a bus appeared around the corner. They were still a couple hundred meters away.

"Give me your bag," he said. "We have to run."

Anna felt a bead of sweat drip down her back and shook her head. "No way. Not in this heat." But she handed over her duffel bag anyway, thankful for the lightening of her load and a bit offended he hadn't offered sooner.

He took the bag and sped up. "No, really, we have to run or we'll miss the bus!"

"Then we'll catch the next one!"

"No, we won't," he said insistently. "There isn't another one for over an hour, and I am not waiting around until then." And then he took off running as the bus stopped, leaving Anna behind.

Anna pulled her small suitcase up by the handle and started running after him. She wasn't about to walk – or wait, for that matter – by herself in this heat.

The people who had been waiting by the stop were

pushing onto the bus at an impressive rate, and Anna wished they'd get on more slowly to buy her some time. The man who was escorting her had already disappeared into the crowd, but Anna was still too far away. She pushed herself as fast as her legs could move her, her suitcase awkwardly bashing against her side with every step. She ignored it, willing herself forward. She had to make this bus.

But she wasn't so lucky. When she was still fifty meters away at least, the bus pulled away, leaving behind it a cloud of dust.

Anna stopped running and bent over, half in devastation at missing the bus and half to catch her breath. She couldn't believe he had left her alone after specifically telling her she couldn't navigate it alone! She also had no idea where to go next. He even had one of her bags. She pulled her phone out of her purse and checked her cell signal. Despite having full bars at the airport, out here there was basically nothing. Not enough to pull up directions to the house, anyway. She was officially stranded.

But as the cloud of dust cleared, she saw a figure standing by the bus stop, holding a pink duffel bag. It was her escort.

"You waited for me!" she called, amazed but smiling, then noticed his face was stern.

"You made us miss the bus," he said, his frown set so deeply that Anna now couldn't picture a different facial expression on him.

She opened her mouth to apologize, but he pushed past her and began walking down the road, leaving her duffel bag behind. Anna grabbed it and followed, struggling once again to keep up.

After half a mile, she began to realize that they were going to walk *all* the way to the house like this. She called out a couple of times to ask for help with her bags, but her escort continued to ignore her, keeping twenty meters or so between them, even when she tried to close the gap. So all Anna could do was trudge on.

Nearly an hour later, Anna scowled as they arrived at a big resort. Her escort still hadn't given a word of instruction. He just strolled through the automatic glass doors and across the marbled floor to reception, whispering something to the young man behind the counter before disappearing down a hallway. This couldn't be right.

The man at the desk looked at Anna expectantly. She walked up to the large counter, which looked like it was made out of driftwood, set her handbag down on it and dropped her duffel bag and suitcase at her feet.

"Are you here to check in?" the man asked.

"No, I'm looking for my grandfather Christos Xenakis. Does he..." Anna looked around, hesitant to ask what seemed like a silly question. "...does he live here?"

The man sneered. "Christos is a worker. A builder. Right now, he will be in the staff room, having lunch. It's just down that hallway, last door on the right." He pointed to an open door behind him to the left, beyond which a hallway stretched. The hallway down which her escort had disappeared.

"Can I leave my bags here?"

"Sorry," he said, "bag drop is for guests only." Then he picked up a walkie talkie off the desk and walked away.

What is it with nobody wanting to help me today? Anna thought. She put her handbag over her shoulder, picked up her suitcase and duffel bag, and headed toward the door. But as she came around the desk, a short Greek man came through the doorway and locked eyes with her. He had thick eyebrows, leathery skin and a giant handlebar mustache. He would have looked like a cartoon villain if it weren't for the broad grin that was getting bigger the closer he got.

"Anna!" he shouted – loud enough that some other people in the lobby turned to look – and wrapped her in a hug, her hands still clutching her suitcase handles. This must be her grandfather. She wondered again how he knew she was coming.

"Hi, Christos," she said, letting go of her bags and lightly patting his back.

After what Anna felt was a few seconds too long, he finally released her. He furrowed his brow and stared at her, and she touched her face to make sure there wasn't anything on her to make him look so concerned.

"You..." he started, closing his eyes as if to focus more. Anna realized he was simply struggling to find the right words in English. "You eat?" he finally managed, petting his stomach to emphasize his meaning.

"No, I haven't," Anna said, shaking her head to make sure he could understand.

He smiled at her and grabbed her bags, nodding for her to follow as he headed back down the corridor.

As they went, Anna realized that she was actually quite hungry. She could go for a gyro or some hummus, or whatever Greek people actually ate for lunch? There was the smell of something delicious on the air, and it seemed familiar, though Anna couldn't quite place it. Maybe it was something from her childhood?

As they walked through the doors, someone threw a small white package at Christos, and he dropped one of Anna's bags to catch it. Anna looked around to see what was going on and spotted a young man throwing things to people all over the room out of a brown paper bag.

A brown paper bag with a big yellow "M" on it.

Of course she would come halfway around the world and still not be able to escape McDonald's. Every man in the room – and they were all men – was now biting into a burger or eating fries from the distinctive red cardboard holder. Not quite what she would have imagined, but it explained the familiar smell at least, a smell now accompanied by sweat and paint.

The men were all dressed the same with the same complexion: hair so dark it was almost black, olive skin, and dark eyes with long, luscious lashes. There were a couple who were middle-aged or older like her grandfather, but the rest were all young and muscular and looked like they should be in an Olympic God of the Month calendar. She was the only woman in a room full of Adonises – not that she was complaining. But as they started to notice her, she saw that their gazes were less flirtatious, not even curious, but more annoyed. The way she would look at tourists who walked too slowly on the sidewalk in Manhattan.

From across the room, she saw her escort amidst the mass of white tee shirts, leaning against the wall and laughing at something one of the other guys had said. He was holding a burger, and, as he took a massive bite out of it, he caught her eye and winked. She felt herself tense everywhere, and her cheeks went red. She tried to remind herself of the ordeal she had endured at his hand to get here, but still she smiled when he started walking toward her.

"Hungry?" he asked as he walked up, grabbing a spare burger the delivery guy had left on the table and offering it to her.

She hadn't eaten McDonald's since she was a kid; her father had taken her after school a few times, but her mother had forbidden it once he'd left, and the habit had stuck once she'd moved to Manhattan. Plus, who needed fast-food restaurants when there was a twenty-four-hour falafel cart less than a block from her building? But she *was* hungry, so she took the burger from him and unwrapped it, relishing the smell of the salty beef as it hit her nose.

"It's the least you can do," she said before sinking her teeth into the burger.

"What do you mean?"

"You made me drag my bags all the way across the island, ignoring me the whole time," she replied, her mouth full. "If I hadn't been able to keep up, I would still be lost out there."

He rolled his eyes. "First of all, the airport is not on the other side of the island. Second, you made it just fine, didn't you?"

"No thanks to you," she said, but she smiled despite herself. "I'm Anna," she said, sticking out her hand.

"I know, I picked you up from the airport," he said, shaking his head.

Anna retracted her hand. "I remember, but I was giving you a chance to introduce yourself properly."

"Ah, okay," he said, wiping his hand on his pants before extending it. Based on their state, Anna wasn't sure it would do any good. "Nikolas Doukas."

Anna swapped her burger to her left hand and shook Nikolas's hand with her right. She felt the same tension as she had at the airport, but she managed to shake hands fairly naturally this time. "Nice to meet you, Nikolas," she replied, trying her best to emulate the accent in which he pronounced his name.

He chuckled in response.

"What?"

"For someone who's half-Greek, your accent is terrible," he said.

"Well, what am I supposed to do about that?"

"You can call me Nikos. Everybody else does."

"Nikos," she said, much more naturally. "How's that?"

"Much better." He was still holding her hand, and he shook it again. "Listen, I'm sorry I didn't help you with your bags. Here in Greece, our women can carry their own luggage."

"Yeah, because Greece is so famous for its progressive feminism," Anna said, rolling her eyes.

"Yeah, well, we're making up for lost time," Nikos said, tilting his head. "You're here about the summer house, right?"

"Yeah, just to get it signed over and maybe on the market."

Nikos chuckled. "On the market? In a week? You'll certainly have your work cut out for you."

"What's that supposed to mean?"

"You'll see," Nikos said with a dismissive wave. "Tomorrow is my day off. I'll come by and help you out."

Anna nodded. "I don't know how much help I'll need, but sure. You can make up for today."

Nikos laughed and nodded. "I have to get back to work in a moment, but help yourself to some more food. Kostas brought more than enough with him." Then he touched her lightly on the shoulder and left.

Alone now, she looked around her, seeing people's eyes flicker over to her and then away again. She leaned against the wall eating her burger, but no one came to speak to her. In fact, people actively avoided her as they moved around the room, giving her a wide berth.

A woman came through the door, a Serious Business Woman with a white blouse, stilettos and a power-bob haircut. She looked around the room, greeting some of the guys, then spotted Anna.

"Hello," she said, walking up with her arm outstretched. Anna set her burger down to shake her hand. "I'm Xenia."

"Anna Linton."

"Nice to meet you, Anna. What are you doing in my staff room?"

Anna looked around. "I'm here with my grandfather," she said, "Christos Xenakis. Nikos brought me here."

"Oh, you're Giorgos's daughter!" she said, smiling. "I heard you were coming. Welcome to Santorini, and to Kamari Sands Resort."

"Thanks, it's my first time here," she said. "Are you the manager here?"

"I own it, actually. Family business. Just bringing it into the twenty-first century, which is why these guys are here." She gestured to the workmen all around the room.

"Nice," Anna said. "Very impressive."

"So, what brings you to the island for the first time?"

"Well…" Anna said, rubbing her hands together, "how much do you know about my parents?"

"Not much," Xenia said, shaking her head. "I mean, I knew your dad, but only casually."

"Well, my parents met here while my mom was traveling, then she got pregnant and they moved back to Connecticut, where my mom is from. My mom had my sister and then me, and Giorgos had a string of affairs, so my mom kicked him out and he lost his green card. When he died a few months ago, he left me and my sister his house, apparently. So I'm here to sell it."

Xenia nodded and inhaled sharply. Anna had definitely given too much information, but she wasn't sure when she'd have another opportunity to talk to someone from Santorini who wasn't already on Giorgos's side.

"Question for you," Anna said, changing the subject. "Does everyone speak such good English? Nikos does too, but not my grandfather."

Xenia shrugged. "It differs, but Nikos and I both went abroad for college. I went to Dartmouth in New Hampshire, and he went somewhere in the UK, I think."

Anna nodded, stifling a yawn; she would have to get a nap in at some point.

"You'll be fine," Xenia said with a smile. "Besides, your grandmother's English is excellent. Now don't hold off on your lunch on my account. I'll see you later."

"Thanks, see you later," Anna said as Xenia left. The guys were starting to filter out, so she grabbed a seat at the table and ate the rest of her burger. There was an order of fries on there, too, so she ate that as well. Afterwards, she sat there for another fifteen minutes or so until her grandfather walked back into the room.

"Anna!" he shouted, just like he had when he first saw her. She would have to get used to that. "You eat?"

Anna nodded. "Yes, yes, I ate," she replied, getting up and walking over to him. "Now where is your home?" she asked, putting both her arms over her head like a roof when he frowned, clearly not getting it. Finally, his eyes lit up with understanding.

"Home!" he said, just as enthusiastically as he had said her name. "Wait," he added, holding up both hands, and left the room again.

Already getting used to her grandfather's disappearing/ reappearing acts, Anna decided she would simply wait for him to return again. So, as the room fully emptied of Greek men, leaving behind wrappers and bags and stray fries, Anna sat back down at the table and put her head down.

An undetermined amount of time later, a hand shook Anna awake.

"Who's there?" she asked, opening her eyes and looking around, feeling a throbbing pain in her neck. How long had she been asleep? As she turned, she saw a woman, maybe in her sixties or seventies, stood behind her with her arms folded across her chest. She wore a navy floral dress with a wide collar and a white apron tied around her plump waist. Her greying hair was secured in a bun with a pencil. She looked like every grandmother from every storybook ever. Which was fitting, since Anna knew from Lizzy's photos that this woman was her grandmother.

"Hi, Eirini," Anna said, unsure of how much she would understand. "We go home?"

"Yes, we've been ready to go for twenty minutes now," she said, surprising Anna with her perfect English. "Christos is more patient than I am. If you're coming with us, please do so now."

Anna nodded, standing up, grabbing her bags and following Eirini back down the corridor and out the front door. The sun was now low in the sky; Anna must have napped for hours. No wonder her neck hurt. A white pickup truck sat just outside, with Christos in the driver's seat. Eirini motioned to the back, where tools and building materials crowded the bed.

"You want me to sit back there?" Anna asked, peering over the edge and trying to find an empty spot big enough for her to sit.

"No, of course not. Just throw your bags in the back and sit between Christos and me." Eirini sighed and stood with the door open.

Anna smiled feebly and nodded, placing her duffel and her roller bag as carefully as possible in the back, but a tool fell loose anyway and clattered about a bit. Anna looked up at Eirini, who was rolling her eyes at Christos.

Eirini then ushered Anna into the cab of the truck, squeezing in next to her, pushing her further and further across the bench until she was pressed up against Christos, who just smiled at her with both his hands on the steering wheel.

As they pulled away from the resort, Anna saw the view out over the island for the first time. She could now see clearly the roads of Kamari that had walled her in before, all of them pointing toward the azure sea. It wasn't the Santorini she had pictured, with winding paths that cut between white stone houses with domed blue roofs that blended in with the sky. But as they wound through farmland and vineyards, she thought it was beautiful nonetheless. She wondered what the view would be like from the summer house. And as they started up a hill and the airport came into view in the distance, Anna remembered how she had ended up in Santorini to begin with.

Four days earlier, Manhattan

Until that moment, the worst moment of Anna's life had been the night just after New Year's when she'd found out her father had died. Her mother had mentioned it in passing, right in between a summary of the previous weekend's yoga retreat and an interrogation of Anna's dating life. The news that her father, the man who had given her life, had dropped dead of a heart attack was apparently on the same level as how well the other middle-aged faux yogis could hold a downward dog.

Not that they had been close, of course, Anna and her father. At least not recently. He had left when Anna was six, riding away in a taxi as Anna's mother had screamed down the street after him, yelling all sorts of names and insults, the white of her satin robe fluttering in the darkness as the wind caught it and tore it open. Anna's big sister, Lizzy, eight at the time, held Anna close as she watched from the window and called down to her mama.

Lizzy thought Anna was screaming because she was sad and scared but, really, she just wanted to tell her mother that her robe was open, and neighbors were starting to peek through their windows at the commotion. She had wondered for twenty years how someone could be so angry and embarrassed and in pain that they stood in the street with a boob out without realizing it.

But now, as Anna stood on Fifth Avenue, looking up at the third-story window of the man who was both her boss and her lover and saw another woman pressed against it, him behind her, both of them naked, faces twisted up in passion and agony and pleasure, Anna understood. She could be in a bathrobe, flapping open in the breeze, the whole of Manhattan staring at her, and she wouldn't be able to think anything but, "You fool. You fool, you fool, you ABSOLUTE FOOL." Like a mantra of disbelief, it kept coming.

She was devastated, but not for the reason she should have been. Marcus, the man she had been seeing for over a year, was fucking another woman right in front of her. Unknowingly, of course, but that didn't make it any less jarring. But staring up at their bodies squished against the window, leaving sweat marks on the glass, she felt defeated. She felt worthless. She didn't mean anything to him. She had had no delusions of romance, but it wasn't until that moment that she understood exactly what she was to him: convenient.

When Anna had been five years old, she'd been chosen as the "Model Student" of her kindergarten class for the

month of May. This meant that she was kind to her class-
mates, did well on assignments, and was the first to
volunteer for things. To be honest, she wasn't actually that
social; she was quite shy, even as a child. A new Model
Student was chosen every month, and there were only
twelve children in her class. Eliminate the ones who got
in trouble a lot, and Anna was pretty much guaranteed
the title at some point in the year, regardless of how bold
or social she actually was.

But that didn't matter to five-year-old Anna. She brought
her shiny yellow ribbon home that day and presented it
proudly to her parents as she walked through the front
door after school. Her father, Giorgos – the girls called
him Baba, but their mother always introduced him as
George – scooped her into a hug and tossed her in the air,
spinning her around and cheering. Grace, Anna's mother,
simply said "well done" and poured herself another glass
of wine.

Anna asked if she could hang the ribbon on the refrigerator, but her mother said that that space was only for
important things to remember. Giorgos had looked coolly
at his wife, but then nuzzled Anna's hair and smiled. "What
your mother means, my darling, is that the refrigerator is
for boring things, and your award is anything but boring.
Why don't we go hang it somewhere in your room?"

The next morning, Anna's mother had left for work
without saying a word to any of them. Giorgos had piled
Anna, Lizzy, and their school things into his painter's van

like always to take them to school. But when they got there, he'd told Anna to stay put; that he wanted to talk to her.

"Baba, what's wrong? Am I in trouble?" Anna asked, watching her sister walk into the building.

But as soon as Lizzy was inside, Giorgos took Anna to the local breakfast chain for as many chocolate chip pancakes as she could handle. "Model Students get celebratory breakfasts," he said, taking a bite of his short stack and putting his arm around Anna, who was sat on the stool next to him, still barely able to reach the counter. As he chewed, a bit of syrup dripped out of his mouth and down his face. Anna pointed and laughed. Her father pretended to be confused before leaning in and planting a big kiss on Anna's cheek, rubbing the syrup in and tickling her with his beard.

After they ate, Giorgos drove Anna back to school and dropped her off at the front door with a note saying she had been at a dentist appointment. Anna was about to ask why they were lying if Model Students were allowed celebratory breakfasts, but when she looked up at her Baba, he looked so sad, so she just gave him a hug and a kiss on the cheek and went inside.

A couple of weeks later, just after Anna's sixth birthday, Giorgos was kicked out of the house, and Lizzy held Anna back as they watched from the window. Their mother would cite this incident of skipping school, alongside temperamental outbursts and a string of affairs she had discovered, in the ensuing divorce and custody battle that would result in Giorgos being sent back to Greece. Grace had never taken the last name Xenakis, and as soon as the divorce was finalized, she changed her daughters' names to Linton to match her own. Anna and Lizzy would never see their father again.

Anna had a difficult time coming to terms with her father's infidelity. It didn't make sense to her. "Baba loves us," she told her mother. "He would never do anything like that. He would never hurt us."

"You're a child," Grace had said. "One day, you'll understand just what a man will do, and then they'll never be able to surprise you with how terrible they can be. But until then, you'll just have to trust me."

Standing on the sidewalk outside Marcus's apartment, her mantra repeating in her mind, Anna finally understood what her mother meant. She did not love this man. She did not have a family with him. But as she watched him through the window, as she felt her world crumbling around her, she began to feel, for the first time, as her mother must have felt: discarded.

Half an hour later, Anna slammed her bedroom door shut and slumped against it, the tears finally coming. She had probably woken her roommate, but she didn't care. She had been fighting back the tears the entire subway ride home, and she was at her breaking point. She tried and failed to push out of her mind the image of what she had seen, but it stayed front and center as she wept.

It wasn't even the fact that Marcus was sleeping with someone else. Anna had known as soon as she started seeing him that their relationship wasn't a monogamous thing. It had been borderline cliché, the way they had hooked up at an opening just over a year before. She had been working at the gallery for months, but it was the first time she had spoken to Marcus, the gallery's owner and world-famous photographer. Well, as world-famous as a photographer could be, anyway. To Anna, who had studied photography in college and been working for years trying to get a job at a gallery, he may as well have been Chris Hemsworth. She nearly died when he walked up to her at the event, and within a couple of hours they were in a hotel room.

No, the awful thing for Anna had been watching her future crumble with every thrust. Anna was just a gallery assistant, and one with ambitions to become a photographer at that. Girls like her were a dime a dozen for Marcus. And despite the fact that she had worked for years to get a job at MarMac, if she wasn't useful to him anymore, she would simply be cast aside for the next girl waiting in the wings. At least, that's what she feared. After a few minutes, Anna crawled up onto her bed, settling on top of a pile of clean laundry, tears still streaming down her cheeks, images of that woman's boobs pressed against Marcus's window burned into her mind, and cried herself to sleep.

Anna awoke what felt like seconds later to find her elbow buzzing. As she opened her eyes, she was confused to find that the sun was streaming brightly through the window, and she quickly snapped them shut again. The buzzing stopped for a few seconds and then started up again. Anna used the hand that wasn't pinned underneath her body to feel around on the bed for her phone. She dug through the pile of clothes and pulled it out, swiping to answer her sister's call.

"It's so early," she said with a croak. "What do you want?"

"Nice to talk to you, too, dear sister," Lizzy said, barely audible over the noise of other people talking and what sounded like cutlery scraping against crockery. Anna could imagine the mess hall of the farm as it had been the one time she'd visited: crowded and sparse, but full of suspiciously happy people. "And it's nearly nine, Banana. Not exactly the wee hours of the morning."

Anna jumped a bit at the realization of what time it

29

was, but them images of what she had seen last night came back to her, and she instantly lost all motivation to go into work.

"Hey, that's still early for some people. What do you want?"

"Touchy, touchy." The noise behind Lizzy died down as she presumably stepped outside. "You okay, sis? You sound like you've been up all night crying."

Anna knew there was no point hiding anything from her sister, but she didn't want to get into it with her. She had somehow managed to keep it from Lizzy that she had been seeing her boss for the last eighteen months. "Not all night," she said, "but I don't really want to talk about it. What's up?"

"Well, it's probably better that you're not at work now," Lizzy replied. "I have some news."

Anna sat up and swung her legs over the side of the bed, her breathing shallow. Those were the four most terrifying words in her sister's vocabulary. "What happened?"

"Well," she said, "some lawyers called from Greece."

"Greece?" Anna asked. "You mean Santorini?"

"Well, actually, the law firm is based in Athens. But yes, it was about Dad."

Anna took a deep breath in. Talking about her dad was not what she needed this morning. "And?"

"And it turns out we have a bit of an inheritance on our hands."

"What kind of inheritance?" Okay, this was actually

possibly good news. Anna's mind immediately went to all the things she could do with inheritance money. But as quickly as the visions of buying a loft apartment and a shopping spree on Fifth Avenue and a first class ticket to a far-off destination came into her mind, they were replaced with a feeling of resentment for her father.

"A house," Lizzy said. "In Santorini."

"I think it's *on* Santorini," Anna said reflexively. "Santorini is an island."

"That doesn't even remotely matter," Lizzy said. "The point is that you and I now share a house in Greece."

"How much is it worth?" Anna asked, apparently too quickly.

"How is that your first question, Anna?" Lizzy asked, her voice raising. "Not about Dad, or why he left it to us? Not even 'when can we go there on vacation?'"

"Sorry," Anna said with a laugh. "But you know I'm not the number-one fan of Greek exports, so I doubt I'll be headed there on vacation any time soon."

Anna swore she could hear a wicked grin in Lizzy's voice as she responded. "That's just it, baby sis. Looks like you'll be going there sooner than expected."

"What? Why?"

"One of us has to go accept the inheritance in person."

"To Athens?"

"No, actually to Santorini. There's a Greek law that says you have to accept real estate in front of a notary public in the region where the property is."

"So one of us has to go to Santorini. Why does it have to be me? Why can't you go?"

Lizzy sighed. "I really wish I could, Anna. You know how much I've wanted to go back since Dad's funeral. But it's asparagus season, so I can't."

Anna couldn't believe what she was hearing. "Asparagus season?" she said, almost shouting. "Are you kidding me? You want me, the one who didn't even go to Greece for her own father's funeral, to go now because you have to harvest some asparagus?"

"Anna, that's not fair," Lizzy said. "You know I'm responsible for the well-being of this farm."

"It's a cooperative farm! You don't even get paid!" Anna was definitely shouting now. "Surely, it's not the end of the world if you take a few days off to do something this important."

Lizzy was quiet for a moment, then responded softly. "I'm really sorry, Anna. I know how much you hated Dad and everything to do with him. But for us to get the house, you have to go accept it.

"As for the farm, I hope that one day you understand what it's like to be a part of a community – a family – that has each other's backs. But, until then, don't pretend to know what sort of obligation I should or should not feel to the people here."

She was quiet for a long time, but eventually Lizzy sighed, and Anna knew then that she wasn't too angry.

"I'm sorry, Liz. I didn't mean to get mad. I just don't want to go. I know you'd like to have a vacation home in Greece, but that's just not important to me. Plus, I have work. And it'll take me months to accrue more vacation time."

"I'm sure if you ask your boss and explain the situation he'd let you have the time. He likes you, doesn't he? What's his name? Martin?"

"Marcus," Anna said, wincing as she said his name. "I don't know, Liz."

"I'll tell you what..." Lizzy said. "If you go there for a week and still hate it, we can sell the house. How does that sound?"

Anna cringed at the idea of having to spend a week in her father's house, interacting with his family, sleeping in his bed. It felt weird after hating him for so long. "I don't know. I'll have to think about it, okay?"

"That's all I ask," Lizzy said over the sound of a bell in the background. "Now I have to go. That's last call for breakfast. But let me know soon. There's a bit of a deadline on us accepting, and the grandparents are not making it easy for us. I don't think they expected anyone other than Dad to ever have it."

"Okay. Good to know, thanks. Love you."

"Love you, too. Bye, Banana."

Anna held the phone up for several seconds after the call disconnected, so unsure of what to do that she felt paralyzed. But regardless of her family drama and what happened with Marcus, she did still have to go to work, so she got up and got dressed. She took noticeably less care with her appearance than usual, which was saying something. She pulled on the first clothes she could find and caught the subway to work.

The entire commute, she bounced back and forth between wondering if she should go to Greece and wondering if she should confront Marcus. On the one hand, she didn't want anything to do with her cheating father's legacy and, regardless of their relationship, Anna felt hurt by what she saw at Marcus's the night before. On the other hand, surely her dad owed her at least this, and Marcus hadn't really done anything wrong since they weren't technically exclusive. The two issues swirled around in her head as she emerged in SoHo and walked up the steps to the MarMac gallery.

As she walked in, she was almost immediately greeted by one of the other assistants, who threw a thumb drive at her that she barely caught.

"These are the early entries for the Emerging Talent contest. Marcus wants us to screen them as they come in so there aren't hundreds of entries for him to go through all at once. And make them anonymous; he wants to be able to tell his sister that the reason her kid didn't win is because he's a shit photographer, not because he's trying to mess with her."

Anna nodded and turned the thumb drive over in her hand as she walked up the stairs to the office. A couple of years ago, she would have jumped at the chance to enter something like this. Even though there were dozens of contests young photographers could enter, Marcus's was special in that it usually resulted in the winner actually gaining momentum in the art world. She even had a collection she had shot just before starting at the gallery that she knew Marcus would like; a series of photos of forgotten Manhattan landmarks. But she was a gallery assistant now, not a photographer. And she worked for Marcus. She couldn't enter.

She sat down at an open desk and looked out over the gallery below. A buyer was there already, someone she recognized from previous events. Rumor had it that Blake Lively and Ryan Reynolds were her clients. As the gallery manager shook her hand and put a sold sticker next to the painting, Anna wished, not for the first time, that her photos could be seen by so many influential people. Almost everyone who showed at MarMac went on to do well. But instead she was sat behind the desk trying to anonymize Marcus's nephew's contest entry.

Anna took out her laptop, connecting to the server and opening up her email like she did every morning. An email came in from Marcus almost immediately.

U ok?

She looked up toward his office, where she could see him peeking through the window.

Not really, she typed out, but she couldn't press Send. It didn't feel right to confront him.

Instead, she stood up to go to the bathroom, avoiding looking toward Marcus's office on her way. As she passed through the door that separated the gallery from the office, she turned her un-made-up face away from the couple of people coming through the front door, walking as quickly as she could across the marble floor.

Once she made it to the Ladies' room, Anna leaned over the sink and splashed cold water on her face. What would she say to Marcus? She was notoriously bad at lying; Lizzy used to clean her out of her Halloween candy when they played poker as kids. Her blushing usually gave her away. Could she manage to get through a work day with Marcus without bringing up what she had seen the night before?

But she didn't have time to figure that out, because the door to the bathroom creaked open, and Marcus poked his head through, stepping in once he saw that Anna was alone.

Standing in front of him, it was easy for Anna to understand how she had fallen under Marcus's spell. He had a universal appeal, looking rugged yet refined at the same time. On the rare occasions he had taken Anna somewhere public, women and men alike would stare at him and shoot daggers at her.

But now, Anna was the one shooting daggers, hard as she tried not to give too much away.

"You want to tell me what's going on?" Marcus said, the slight southern draw that Anna was pretty sure was an affectation coming out strong.

"What are you talking about?"

Marcus smiled and looked at his feet. "I'm talking about you coming into work nearly two hours late looking like you got hit by a bus. I know you're sleeping with the boss, but you wouldn't want to appear to be taking advantage."

Anna felt her stomach churn. Normally, she would have laughed it off, but she had too much on her mind to make the effort. "Are you kidding me?" she asked. "I've never asked you for a thing, especially not since our little arrangement began. Excuse me for having a bad day."

Marcus's smile dropped, and he stepped toward Anna, rubbing his hands up and down her arms. "Hey, hey, what's going on? I didn't mean to offend you."

"I'm fine," she said. She opened her mouth to say more, but she felt the truth of last night bubbling inside her, so she shut it tight.

"You know you can tell me anything, right, Anna?" he asked, condescension dripping from his words, as if she were a little girl trying to hide that she had eaten the last cookie.

"Is that what you said to the girl you fucked last night?" She felt the words tumble out of her mouth, trying and failing to catch them and shove them back in. So much for not confronting him. Marcus gave very little away, but she could tell from the twitch in his eye that she had surprised him.

"You were at the theater?"

"No, I was at your apartment. Or, I was on my way there

when I saw you through the window." *Though nice to know you were flaunting her around at the theatre, too.*

Marcus was quiet for a moment, then his eyes widened as he realized what she must have seen. Then, just as quickly, he was back on his game. "Anna, I'm sorry that you saw that, but surely you didn't think you were the only person I was dating?" He was digging in his heels; asserting his dominance. He must have thought so little of her.

She realized in that moment just how disposable she was to him. And as long as she was disposable, she was never going to get anywhere working for him. If she had felt discarded last night, she felt absolutely disintegrated now. She needed to figure something else out.

"Marcus, I need to take some time off," she said.

"Great," he said. "Submit your vacation request to HR for approval."

"No," she said, "I have to go now. I have nearly three weeks of paid vacation accrued. I'll be taking it now. When there are two weeks left, I'll send in my notice."

He frowned at her. "So much for not taking advantage of the situation."

She glared at him. "I'm not taking advantage. My dad died a few months ago, and he left me a property in Greece. I have to go there to claim it. I only have a small window before it goes to someone else, so I have to go now."

"You have to go on vacation urgently enough that you're willing to quit this job?" He laughed. "Are you kidding?"

"Nope. Not kidding," she said, shaking her head. "And it's not a vacation. I've just explained the situation."

He nodded slowly. "I hope you know that you've just ruined your future," he said, but Anna saw a flicker of hurt cross his face, and she felt a tiny spark of pride that she had taken back control – she'd hurt him before he could hurt her again.

Without saying another word, he slipped through the door and was gone, leaving Anna standing there alone, her hands still dripping with water.

She kept staring at the door for a good minute after he left. How had her frustration with Marcus turned into a decision to go to Greece? But she had said it, and she couldn't take it back. She wouldn't grovel for her job back. She wasn't about to let Marcus think she was taking advantage of their arrangement. Not after this.

She dried her hands, pulled her phone out of her pocket and texted Lizzy:

You win. I'll leave in a couple of days

It looked like Anna was going to Santorini, whether she liked it or not.

Santorini

The front of the house was positively quaint, Anna thought. It was nestled between two hills in a sort of mini valley. Three white stone arches covered in vines framed a door in the center and two windows, one on each side. A stone wall extended from each side of the front, with a gate several meters to the left and another beyond that. Anna walked through the center archway, looking around as she went. The front of the house was covered in climbing vines, crowded at the bottom by weeds. The wooden front door was beautiful and weathered; it looked like it had been there for hundreds of years, but it was still strong and sturdy.

Eirini called for Anna to follow her through the first gate, bringing her into a square courtyard, about fifteen feet on each side with a table in the middle. The walls were covered in the same climbing vines as the front of the house, nearly obscuring the white paint underneath.

As she followed Eirini through the next gate to the back garden, Anna found herself looking at the most beautiful little cottage she could imagine. It was made of the same whitewashed stone, but it was covered in gorgeous pink flowers. It was small -- Anna imagined it couldn't have been more than one or two rooms -- but it was the kind of place that Anna would have booked immediately if she'd found it online.

"Is that...?" Anna pointed at the cottage and looked at Eirini, not wanting to make another mistake but hoping dearly that this was the summer house.

"This is your father's cottage," she said, "so, yes, I guess it is legally yours now. For some reason."

Anna ignored the last part and walked up to the cottage, peeking through the window next to the door. It was dirty, but she could see a bed, and another door further on. She turned around to look at the garden, but she couldn't see where the entrance was. "How do you get back here?"

Eirini sighed. "You can go through the courtyard, or you can use the far gate. But that's difficult to get to. You will need to put in a path, eventually. The courtyard is the only part of our property you have access to."

Anna nodded in understanding. She wasn't about to try to cross this woman, though she would have to see about getting that path put in. Maybe a fence between the houses as well.

Eirini extended a set of keys to Anna, so she moved a

few steps closer to her and took them. With that, Eirini turned around and walked back into the house, closing the door behind her.

Christos was sticking his head around the door from the courtyard, and he stepped into the garden after Eirini had gone. "Is Giorgos house," he said, slowly and deliberately. "Eirini love Giorgos... very much. Is hard." And then he turned and followed Eirini inside.

Anna watched her grandfather go inside, wishing he spoke better English so she could avoid Eirini. She turned around to inspect her new home, and as she saw it she felt giddy yet again. This would definitely make a great rental property. Maybe there was a rental agency they could work with, and they wouldn't have to sell it. Then she and Lizzy could come whenever they wanted, and...

...and nothing. After her icy reception from Eirini, Anna knew that she would never be welcome here. She would have to part with the summer house. But that didn't mean she couldn't enjoy a few days in it. She'd just have to find somewhere to spend her time where she could fit in with the other tourists.

Anna unlocked the door and went inside. As she had expected, it was just one big room with a bathroom in the corner. It was immediately obvious, however, that it was in no state to rent out or sell as it stood. The small kitchen in the far-right corner was filled with rust-covered appliances, and one cabinet door was hanging by a hinge. The mattress on the bed looked like ones Anna had seen in back alleys in Manhattan. The wooden floor was almost completely covered in a thick layer of dust. And while the bathroom had a lovely freestanding tub in it, there was no flooring and no sink. This must have been what Nikos meant when he said she wouldn't have it on the market in a week. The summer house was going to need a lot of work. She just had to determine if that work was her responsibility.

Anna pulled out her phone to ring Lizzy, and, after taking a moment to connect to the Greek network, a flood of messages came through. Unable to leave the notifications alone, Anna went through each one: a confirmation that the room she was subletting would be held for her; a text from the pizza delivery near her apartment in New York offering "15% off" for the next three days, and a notification that she had beat Lizzy in their latest round of Words With Friends.

Next, she reluctantly opened her work emails, with the intention of just checking there was nothing important waiting for her, but saw a message from Marcus's assistant waiting in her inbox. The subject line was "Moving forward," so she clicked into it.

Hi, Anna. Due to your recent tardiness, the second documented offense of its kind...

The first had been the morning after she found out her father had died. She had only been twenty minutes late.

As for her second offense, she didn't even realize she had been written up again. The email continued:

> ...we no longer feel you are a good fit for MarMac. We would like to give you your two-week notice, which will begin immediately. We are aware that you are away on personal matters, so while we will pay you for the two weeks, you should consider your employment with MarMac, Inc. to be complete. Please return the attached paperwork in order to be eligible for the next two weeks' pay.

Anna couldn't believe what she was reading. He was firing her before she could send in her notice. This was a new low for Marcus; not content with sweeping Anna under the rug because he was done with her, he had to have the last word, too. She set a reminder for the next morning to fill out the paperwork before tapping out her reply.

> Really classy, Marcus. Thanks for the heads up.

His response came quickly:

> Don't be a child, Anna. At least I gave you severance pay. Just remember that you'll never be a photographer if you can't take your work seriously.

Anna groaned and slammed her phone down. He was *so* infuriating. At least this meant she would be able to stay a bit longer to get the house sold. As she looked around again, she began making a mental list of everything that the new owner would have to do: replace the mattress, tile the bathroom, buy a sink, repair the cabinets, replace the oven, clean the refrigerator, clean the floors, clean the windows... okay, clean everything. And replace a lot of things. Or maybe she was supposed to do all that before putting it on the market? If so, this was going to cost her a lot of time and a lot of money. But, then again, she had a little bit of both to spare.

She picked up her phone again, this time to call Lizzy.

"Hey, Banana!" Lizzy shouted. "You there yet? I was beginning to worry about you."

"Yeah, I'm here," Anna said. "I fell asleep for a while. Sorry. But I'm at the summer house now."

"How was your journey from the airport?" Lizzy asked, and Anna could tell that she was smiling mischievously on the other end of the line.

"Horrible," she said. "Some guy named Nikos picked me up and we had to walk all the way to the resort where Christos works."

"I told him to drive you!"

"You told him?" Anna asked. "How do you know Nikos?"

"I met him at Dad's funeral," Lizzy said. "I thought you might enjoy having him as your escort."

"Very funny," Anna said. "I'm not really in the market for a Greek booty call. A Greek summer house is about all I can handle at the moment."

"Fine, fine, fine," Lizzy relented with a sigh. "And what do you think of the summer house?"

"Well... it definitely has potential..."

"Potential? That's how they describe absolute dumps on home-improvement reality shows!"

"Yeah, well, I think that would be pretty fitting, given that it looks like a crack den at the moment." Anna walked around as she spoke, opening cabinets to get a sense of what was there. She tried not to balk at the state of some of the dishes, but she knew they would be getting thrown out rather than cleaned.

Lizzy sighed. "Oh, Anna, I'm sorry. I really thought it would be in better condition. Eirini and Christos must not have been in there since Dad died."

Anna opened her mouth to respond, but as she did, she saw an air mattress and some bedding in a cabinet that looked decidedly cleaner than everything else she had seen.

"I wouldn't be so sure about that," she said, silently thanking Christos for the fact that she wouldn't have to sleep on the mattress currently on the bed. "But it's nothing I can't handle. I just need to pay to fix it up first..."

"How much are we talking?"

Anna did some quick mental math. "Maybe a couple thousand? I need new furniture, a new oven, a sink for the bathroom, and some tiles for the bathroom floor."

"Anna, that's a lot of money for us," Lizzy said. "Remember, we don't get paid here. Plus, isn't that a lot to do before you have to get back for work?"

"Well, actually," Anna replied, "about that…"

"What happened? Did you get more time off at work?"

"Something like that," Anna said. She didn't want to tell Lizzy she had been fired; that would mean telling her about what had been happening with Marcus. "The point is that I can stay as long as I need to. I've got my savings and a pay check coming through soon. Then I can just recoup the money for the repairs from the sale before we split it."

"That sounds perfect," Lizzy said. "You're the best." Anna could hear noise in the background. "Hey, Banana, I've got to go, but thanks again for handling this. Just remember to have an open mind with Dad's family. There's two sides to every story."

"Yeah, whatever," Anna said, rolling her eyes. That had been Lizzy's line ever since she'd gone to the funeral. But Anna wasn't interested in sides. She was interested in getting out of Greece as soon as possible.

"Let me know what else you need. Love you!"

"Love you, too," Anna said, but the line was already disconnected. She put down the phone and began to roll out the air mattress, but her stomach began to growl. It had been hours since she last ate, she realised. She poked around in the cupboards and refrigerator, but there was nothing to be found. She pulled a granola bar out of her bag but decided to save it for breakfast. She'd need energy if she was going to walk to get food and supplies the next morning.

She plugged in the air mattress and started to inflate it, but it was incredibly slow. So she sat down at the table and opened up a new game of Words With Friends. A few minutes later, the mattress was about two thirds full, and Anna was just playing a very weak "team" onto the game board when she heard a light knock on the door. As she opened it, she saw a bowl of stew and a chunk of bread on a tray on top of a cardboard box. She looked over just in time to see the door to the main house click shut. Anna smiled as she brought the tray inside. She would have to find a way to thank Christos for helping her out. She set it down on the table and went back for the cardboard box. She put it on the bed and opened the top. Inside were a couple of clean glasses, a couple different kinds of towels, a dustpan and brush, a few rags and some bottles of various cleaners. At the bottom there was a note that said keep the dishes.

The air mattress pump started to whine in a slightly higher pitch, and Anna saw that it was full, so she turned it off. Almost immediately, she could hear a faint whistling coming from somewhere. The hole must have been what made it fill so slowly. This was going to be a long night.

Anna sat down and ate the stew. It was one of the best meals she had eaten in ages. It certainly beat the falafel cart down the street from her apartment, and it even beat some of the "fancy" restaurants she had been to with Marcus. She ate as much as she could with the spoon, then she finished the rest with the bread.

When she was done, she pulled a rag and a bottle of dish soap out of the box and washed her dishes in the sink. Then she cleaned the countertop so she would have a clean place to dry her dishes and laid out a towel for them to rest on.

Anna walked into the bathroom, and as she turned the corner she saw that opposite the bathtub was a huge picture window that looked out over the island. She could see from here how high up they were, nestled into the hills they had climbed on the way here. And between two of those hills was just a peek of what Anna knew from a quick check of the map on her phone was the caldera on the other side of the island. Her father must have built the summer house with a window here just so he could get that view, though why he wanted it from the bathroom was beyond her.

The stars were shining in the sky, and Anna took a moment to appreciate that she was as far from home as she had ever been. Lizzy had come back to Greece for their father's funeral, but Anna had elected to stay home rather than grieve the man who had left her as a child. The farthest she had been was to Vancouver with her mother when she was a teenager and Cancun for one spring break. She had been meaning to get out and see the world but living in Manhattan on an assistant's salary was hard. She had barely managed to save the five thousand dollars in her bank account, mostly leftover excess from the student loans she was still paying off. Most months she could barely make her rent, much less buy a transatlantic plane ticket.

And that transatlantic flight was starting to take its toll. Anna slipped the sheet over the air mattress, turning the pump on for a few desperate minutes before bedtime. She didn't have a pillow, so she filled the pillowcase with her softest clothing and tried to nestle in. And despite it being the least comfortable sleeping arrangement she had experienced since slumber parties on the floor as a child, Anna fell asleep as soon as her head hit the makeshift pillow.

5

The next morning, Anna awoke to a knock on the door. She rolled over on the now almost fully deflated air mattress, hair matted and mouth dry, wondering what time it was. The light coming through the window suggested it was fully daytime outside. The heat confirmed her assessment as Anna felt a trickle of sweat roll down her leg.

"Anna," came a muffled voice along with the next knock. "Anna, are you in there?"

She groaned an affirmation, but the person at the door did not hear her. She propped herself up on her elbows and blew a strand of hair out of her face.

"Whoareyouandwhatdoyouwant?" she mumbled, barely able to keep her eyes open. But it did no good. Anna was forced to stand up, adjust her pajamas, and walk over to the door. As she opened it, a far-too-awake Nikos stood in front of her with a cup of coffee in his hand. She took it, shut the door, re-locked it, and went back to the air mattress, her bum touching the floor as she sat down.

"Anna, you have to let me in!" Nikos said through the door.

"Go away!" she shouted with as much volume as she could muster. "It's too early!" Then she pulled the blanket over her head.

She heard the muffled sound of his now-all-too-familiar chuckle. "Early? It's barely even morning anymore."

Anna rolled over and pressed the home button on her phone. The screen said 11:47.

She jolted awake. How could she have slept so late? *Damn jet lag*, she thought.

She shuffled back over to the door and turned the lock, dreading seeing the smug expression on Nikos's face. But as the door opened, he just smiled, not a hint of smugness in sight.

"Tired from the flight?" he asked.

"I guess so."

"Makes sense," he said. He pointed inside. "So, may I come in?"

Anna stepped aside to let Nikos in and shut the door behind him. As he pulled a chair out and sat down in front of the table, Anna walked over to retrieve the coffee he had brought her, then back over to the table, where she sat down opposite him.

"So, did you sleep okay?" he asked.

Anna looked over at the almost-flat air mattress. "Not great," she said, rubbing at her neck. "But anything beats sleeping on that grubby thing." She pointed to the mattress on the bed frame.

"Yeah, your dad had been meaning to replace that. Never got around to it, I guess."

Anna stiffened at the mention of her father. "You knew Giorgos?"

Nikos smiled and looked curiously at her. "You call your dad Giorgos?"

"Well, he wasn't really much of a dad," Anna said as she took another sip and looked down at the table, her lips pursed due partly to the coffee and partly to the subject matter. He had been a fine dad for the first twenty percent of Anna's life. But his record wasn't stellar after that. Non-existent, in fact.

"Not to you, maybe."

Anna looked up, and Nikos was staring back at her with something that looked suspiciously like pity.

"Do you want to tell me why you're here?"

"I'm here to help you," he said. "You want to fix up the summer house, and I'm here to lend a hand."

"Thanks," Anna said, "but I'm not really sure where to start."

"Well, Christos said that we could use his tools, and we have the truck for the day, but you'll have to buy materials," Nikos said, walking around the room. "So why don't you make a list, and I'll meet you around front with the truck?"

She nodded.

"Great. See you out front in five."

As Nikos left, Anna pulled a pen out of her bag. She didn't have any paper, so she tore one of the flaps off the cardboard box and began to make a list as she noticed things:

Mattress
Pillow
Oven
Sink
Plumbing stuff
Tiles for bathroom floor
Curtains
Curtain rods x2
Vacuum
Dishes
Pots, pans & utensils
Place settings
Trash can
Toilet paper
Food
Bathroom toiletries
Paper
Artwork for walls
Bath mat
Laundry hamper
Hangers
Area rug

As Anna made her list, she realized she had gone from trying to get the summer house to be sellable to putting down luxuries; things that would only matter if she were going to stay for longer. She crossed them off the list. She certainly wouldn't need a laundry hamper for just a couple of weeks.

List complete, Anna went outside, to find Nikos speaking with her grandmother at the front of the house by the truck. Eirini was happily chatting to him, but the moment she saw Anna, she dropped her smile and squeezed past into the courtyard.

"Can you believe that?" Anna said, gesturing behind her as she climbed in the truck. "You would think that having her long-lost granddaughter come to visit would be a bit more exciting for her."

Nikos shook his head as he climbed in and started the engine. "It's not you," he said. "It's the situation. None of them knew Giorgos was leaving the summer house to anyone. And it's not like anyone was keeping you away from visiting them before now, were they?"

"That's a bit unfair," Anna said as Nikos reversed down the drive. "Excuse me for not wanting anything to do with the family of the man who cheated on my mother and abandoned his family."

Nikos slammed on the brakes hard enough that Anna was thrown forward in her seat.

"What the hell was that for?" she shouted, turning to him.

"Maybe it's better if we don't talk about Giorgos, okay?" he said, frowning. "I understand why you don't like him based on the story you know, but that wasn't my experience with him, and I won't sit around and listen to you complain about him when you clearly don't know the whole story."

Anna blushed and looked at her lap. She felt she had every right to complain about her father, but maybe she needed to realize that she was the odd one out here. And she didn't want to push Nikos away. She needed his help too much if she was going to get out of Greece as soon as possible.

"Fine," Anna said. "Let's just fix up his summer house and be around his family without ever once mentioning him. Sounds easy." She looked up at Nikos, who was still frowning, and rolled her eyes. "Okay, fine, for real. No Giorgos talk."

Nikos nodded, put the truck back into gear, and started down the road.

"So tell me about yourself, then," he said as they turned onto the main road.

"Not much to tell," Anna said. "I'm from Connecticut, which I'm sure you know from he-who-must-not-be-named. I moved to New York City about a year and a half ago to work at an art gallery. I spend too much time at work, not enough time with my sister, and too much of my salary on cheap wine and falafels. And now I'm halfway around the world collecting inheritance property. Does that about do it?"

"Do you have a boyfriend?" Nikos asked, smiling slyly at Anna.

"No," she said, perhaps a bit too sharply. Nikos noticed.

"Sounds like there's a story there."

"Does it?" She wasn't about to take the bait. "I assure you, there is no boyfriend."

"So when do you have to be back at this art gallery job of yours?" he asked.

"Well, the thing is…" Anna wasn't sure what to say. She hadn't even told Lizzy that she was fired. But was she going to try to convince Marcus to give her her job back? No, the thought of that made her feel sick. So what was the harm in saying so? "I don't really have a job to go back to," she admitted.

"So, your stay is open-ended, then?" Nikos asked, and he almost sounded excited. "Maybe you should see a bit more of the island. Make sure you get the full experience before you go back to the city."

"We'll see," Anna said. "I only want to be here as long as I have to be in order to get the summer house on the market."

Nikos laughed. "I think you'll find that will be much longer than a couple of weeks. We're on island time here, and then there's Greek time on top of that."

"What is Greek time?"

Nikos chuckled again. "Let's just say your social life here will involve a lot of waiting around for people."

Anna shrugged. "We'll see. Plus, I don't think I'll have enough time to develop much of a social life."

"We'll see about that," Nikos said as they turned into a car park. "Okay, first things first, let's get you an actual bed to sleep on."

A couple of hours later, Anna ran out of the McDonald's in Fira with a greasy brown bag and two drinks. They had tried to fit through the drive-through, but Anna's new mattress was sticking up too high, so Nikos had made her run in for the food, his only demand for payment for the day of help.

"Two Big Macs, chicken nuggets with sweet and sour sauce, large fries and a Coke," Anna said, her own burger and fries taking up very little space in the bag. "I still can't believe you can eat that much."

"Seeing is believing," Nikos said. "Now let's get back to your dad's place so you can see."

"It's my place," Anna said quietly.

"What?"

"I said it's my place now," Anna said, louder this time. "I know everyone wishes I would have just stayed away, but it's my place now. And I think I deserve it, what after going without a father for the last two decades."

Nikos sighed as he stared at the road ahead. "I don't think anyone feels that way – that you should have stayed away."

Anna scoffed. "Yeah, right. You're telling me Eirini wouldn't prefer to have her backyard empty of unwanted grandchildren right now?"

He hesitated a beat before responding. "I thought we weren't going to talk about this?"

"Yeah, well, we're not," Anna said, crossing her arms. "But that response does sort of prove my point." *Plus, it's not nice to be completely ignored by your only family for thousands of miles.*

They made the rest of the drive in silence. When they pulled up to the house a few minutes later, Anna took the food and a couple of shopping bags from the back. Nikos grabbed the mattress and lifted it over his head, following behind her.

"You sure you don't want to wait until I can help with that?" Anna asked.

"I'm fine. Just carry the light stuff and leave the heavy lifting to the pros," Nikos said, though Anna could hear a strain in his voice. She just chuckled and continued toward the summer house, leaving the gates open for Nikos behind her. She turned around as she walked through the back gate and chuckled again when she saw him trying to squeeze the mattress down so it would fit through the front gate.

As she walked up to the front door of the summer house, she saw another stew waiting outside for her. She looked from it to the McDonald's bag and felt a small pang of guilt. She hoped Nikos could eat as much as she claimed. She unlocked the door and stepped carefully around the bowl as she went inside, dropping the bags on the table.

Then, behind her, Anna heard the crunch of something

breaking. She turned around to see Nikos frozen, facing away from the door, holding the mattress behind him, the bottom of one of his pant legs soaked in stew, the bowl broken under his boot.

Anna started to laugh.

"Okay, that is not funny," Nikos said, but he started to laugh as well. He picked his leg up to inspect it.

"No, don't move," Anna said between chuckles. "I want to make sure you don't track any shards into the house." She reached into one of the shopping bags and grabbed a rag, the price tag still attached, then started picking up pieces of the bowl and putting them on the tray.

"Smells like carrot," Nikos said, still laughing. "What a shame."

Anna finally managed to pull herself together and began picking shards from the tread of Nikos's boot. As she pulled it closer to get a better look, he nearly fell, only just catching himself with the mattress, and it set the two of them off laughing again.

When they eventually managed to make it into the summer house, Nikos swapped the mattresses and immediately collapsed onto the new one while Anna dealt with the mess.

"Hey, lazy bones, no way. We've still got an oven and a bathroom sink to unload from that truck."

"Come on, Anna, it's nap time. We've worked so hard."

"Not a chance," Anna said, pulling at his arm, but he shooed her away. "I only have two weeks to get this place in working order. I'm not going to waste perfectly good hours of the day resting."

"Says the girl who slept until noon." He didn't move, but instead began pretend-snoring. For just a moment, Anna stood there admiring the sight of him lying on her bed. She didn't hate it. But she shook it off. She had more important things to focus on.

"Fine," Anna said, walking back to the table. "I guess I'll just have to eat all this food myself."

Nikos rolled over and propped himself up on one elbow. "I'd like to see you try."

"I wouldn't have to if you would just come eat," she said, holding an order of fries in front of her, wafting the scent toward him with her hand.

"Fine," Nikos said, hopping up and trying to grab the fries from her hand. But Anna pulled them away.

"Not until you help me bring in the rest," she said.

"But it will be cold by then!" he said, pouting and tilting his head.

"Then maybe you shouldn't have stepped in stew or tried to take a nap."

Nikos groaned. "I knew I shouldn't have let you pay for lunch."

"That's right," Anna said, putting the fries back in the bag and guiding him toward the door. "Now let's go earn it."

6

A couple of days later, Anna and Nikos were stood in line at Vodafone to get Anna a Greek cell phone. She was only going to be in town for a little while, but she had racked up an impressive phone bill for the month of May, so she needed to use a bit less data and make fewer calls. At the moment, she was scrolling obsessively through Instagram while connected to the WiFi, liking all the Memorial Day photos of people in the Hamptons and Nantucket.

"Are those people your friends?" Nikos asked, watching over her shoulder.

"Not really," Anna said. "A couple of them are friends from high school or the city. But most of them are just bloggers and YouTubers."

Nikos rolled his eyes. "I swear, Instagram is the best and the worst thing to ever happen to this island. We're grateful for the business, but it's a pain in the ass to be stopped every few meters in Oia because someone doesn't want any people in their photo stood on top of someone's wall."

Anna laughed. "Tell us how you really feel."

He shot her a look. "Honestly, don't get me started. I could rant about *influencers*" – he made air quotes with his fingers – "all day long."

It was their turn at the counter, so Anna set the flip phone she had chosen in front of her and let Nikos do the talking. She wasn't about to get talked out of all her money because she didn't speak Greek. When Nikos went to pay, Anna tried to press her credit card into his palm, but he shook his head and squeezed her hand in his.

"Why did you do that?" she asked him as they exited the shop, her new flip phone in her purse next to her iPhone.

"Your grandfather saw everything we bought the other day and told me to put anything else you need on the business account."

"What? Really? Why would he do that?" Anna asked, though she knew the answer. She smiled as she thought about how excited he had been to see her.

"Not everyone is as upset as Eirini about a new generation of Xenakises taking up residence in the summer house."

Anna frowned a bit. "My name's Linton," she said, realizing even as she said it how ungrateful she sounded. These people were her family, after all.

Nikos looked at her out of the corner of his eye. Clearly, he was as unimpressed with her comment as she was. "Whatever you are, your grandfather is really excited that you're here. And I think his feelings would be hurt if he heard how quickly you disown his son and his family, two things he's extremely proud of."

Anna looked at her shoes as they walked. She didn't like Nikos chastising her. But when she peeked up at him, he wasn't frowning but smiling softly at her. She returned the smile with her own tentative version.

"That is, if he could understand you to begin with, which would be a miracle," he said, breaking the tension. They laughed together for a moment the unease of his reprimand effectively diffused for the moment. They climbed into the truck, and Anna broached the topic again, less defensively this time.

"So, you knew Giorgos—" Nikos shot her a look from the driver's seat. "Sorry, I mean, you knew my dad well?"

Nikos nodded. "Really well. My father was never in the picture, and my mother died in childbirth. They were really poor, and she couldn't get to a hospital. But my aunt was there, and she raised me along with my cousins, even though she was a single mother as well. When she got sick, I came back from university to help out, and your father convinced your grandfather to give me a job. I had never even held a hammer before, and look at me now."

He grinned and sat up straight, and Anna giggled. Nikos looked over at her and smiled.

"I love your laugh," he said, and Anna felt her face flush immediately.

"You know you do that a lot, right?" he said, his gaze locked on her.

"Do what? Laugh?"

"No, blush when I look at you."

Of course, all this did was make Anna blush even more. She turned away and looked out the window, rolling it down a bit to get some fresh air on her face.

"Anyway," Nikos said, thankfully changing the subject. "Your dad took me under his wing. He trained me, not just at work, but also at home. He taught me how to cook for my aunt and cousins, and he showed me how to budget. He even helped me finish my sustainable agriculture degree online."

"He did?" Anna asked, turning to him. "I wouldn't have thought he would have known about that sort of thing."

"That's just it, he didn't," Nikos said. "He stayed up just as late as I did every night, reading the textbooks and quizzing me on the effect of nuclear power plants on the environment. And when my aunt died and I couldn't get out of bed for days, he logged on and took one of my tests for me. Got an A, too."

Anna looked down at her hands. This sounded like the father she remembered from when she had been little. Caring. Thoughtful. Passionate. Not like the man who had cheated on them and then left. "You make him sound like such a good guy."

"He was," Nikos said firmly. "The best. And an amazing

father, no matter what you think you know. And the day his heart gave out was the saddest day of my life."

Anna had been ordered her whole life to never talk about her father, never to bring him up around her mother, until she didn't want to talk about him either. But now she was a part of his world; living in his house, with his parents. Hanging out with someone he apparently spent so much of his time with. And she found herself growing more and more curious about who he really was.

"Maybe you can tell me more about him sometime," Anna said as they pulled up to the house.

"I'd like that," Nikos said, smiling. He parked the truck and put his hand tentatively on Anna's knee. It was warm, and she could feel his calluses on her skin. She froze at his touch, not ready to reciprocate it but not wanting to scare him off either.

"But for now," he said, moving his hand away, "we have a bathroom to tile!" Then he turned, climbed out of the truck and disappeared through the gate. Anna could still feel where his hand had been on her knee.

Eventually, she got out of the truck and grabbed a pack of tiles from the bed, barely able to lift it herself. As she came through the courtyard, she could hear Nikos arguing with someone up ahead – a woman, in Greek. As she turned the corner, she nearly dropped the tiles on her feet at the sight of one of the most beautiful girls she had ever seen shouting at Nikos. Her hair was so long that a bit of it was caught in the waistband of her jean shorts, the colour the same dark brown as Nikos's. She looked to be around the same age as him. Anna wondered who she was and why they were shouting at each other, but she had a sinking feeling she was walking into the middle of a lovers' quarrel.

The girl caught sight of Anna and smiled deviously. "Oh, now it all makes sense," she said in perfect English.

"I'm sorry," Anna said, "there's really nothing going on between us. Nikos just works for my grandfather, and he was helping me get supplies. Nothing happened, I promise..."

Anna trailed off as she realized Nikos and the mystery woman were laughing.

"Just so we're clear," the girl said, walking toward her, "you think I'm worried the two of you did something because I'm his girlfriend?" She smirked, and Anna felt immediately defensive.

Anna felt her face get hot again. "I mean, yeah... I may not look like you, but it's not like no one has ever been interested in me..."

"Thank god you don't look like her," Nikos said, gently hitting the girl's arm as she doubled over with laughter. Anna's face was practically on fire by now.

"Oh yeah? Why's that?"

"Because it would be weird if I was attracted to my cousin," he said, lifting the tiles from Anna's arms and taking them into the summer house.

"You're his cousin?" she asked the girl. *As in the daughter of his aunt, meaning the person he grew up with, making you basically his sister?*

The girl stepped forward and stuck out her hand. "That's me. Elena."

"I'm Anna." Anna placed her hand in Elena's, feeling strangely relieved. "Wait, so if you're not together, why were you angry with him for hanging out with me?"

"I don't care who Nikos is with," Elena said. "I care that he was meant to drive me to work nearly an hour ago but forgot. Which makes sense now."

Anna furrowed her brow. "It does?"

"Oh yeah," Elena said, walking out toward the truck. "He's definitely got a type. Nice to meet you, Anna." And then she disappeared around the corner.

Anna wondered what that meant. Did Nikos make a habit of getting close with American girls? Maybe his relationship with "influencers" was more complicated than he'd let on.

Nikos walked out of the house and back to Anna. "You okay, Linton?" he asked, showing that he had heard her before, that he was respecting her wishes about her name. "Don't worry, I'll be back in twenty minutes. I'll even unload the rest of the tiles if you get started on the grout."

Anna just nodded. He stopped next to her as he walked past and leaned over. "You're doing it again," he whispered.

She turned to him, her face just inches from his, close enough that she could feel warmth coming off him. "Doing what?"

"Blushing," he replied with a wink, and then he walked away.

Anna stood in place until she heard the truck pull away, and then she went inside and sat down on her bed. She put a hand on her cheek. It was hot, and not just from the Santorini heat.

She opened her phone to text Lizzy about what had just happened, but before she could she noticed she had an email notification waiting. It was from the lawyer managing her father's estate. Anna sighed and opened it up. It was time to stop worrying about men and remember why she was actually here.

Nikos returned half an hour later. "Sorry I was longer than promised," he said as Anna let him in, three boxes of tiles in his hands. Anna saw his eyes flicker from the untouched grout to her computer, open on her bed with the website for a local real estate agent pulled up. "What have you been up to?"

"I checked my email when I got in," she replied. "There was an email from the lawyer. He's coming tomorrow so I can sign the inheritance deed. But apparently we have to pay an inheritance tax on the value of the property, which of course I'm only increasing with every improvement."

"So what does that mean?"

Anna took a deep breath. "It means that we have to wait to do any more work on the house. I need to get it valued in its current state so that the tax is as low as possible, then fix it up before putting it on the market so we can get as much as possible for it. It's going to take ages."

Anna tried to keep breathing deeply, but she was panicking. She had been since she saw the email just a few minutes after Nikos left. If her math was correct, by the time she could get the house on the market, it would be nearly a month from now. And, even then, she'd be lucky if she could get enough to make the inheritance tax and her trip out here feel worth it. It wasn't like she had a job to go back to.

So much for a quick trip.

At least her panic attack had distracted her from Nikos and whatever it was that was happening between them. She did not need that, especially now that she knew she would have to stay a bit longer.

Anna thought about the reception she had received from her grandmother. Even the stews had stopped coming from her grandfather, presumably because he'd seen her carrying in groceries. Nobody wanted her here any more than she wanted to be here. How was she going to stay for a whole month in a place where she didn't have a job, didn't have a car, didn't speak the language and only knew one person who would give her the time of day? She pictured herself trapped in the tiny summer house all alone for a month, and the reality of the situation – everything that had happened with Marcus, losing her job, the inheritance – came crashing down on her. She began to cry.

"Oh, Anna," Nikos said, wrapping her in a hug. "I know

it's difficult. But Christos will help with expenses. I know it's not ideal, but you have people on your side."

Anna pushed him away. "No, don't you get it? I don't." She was surprised to find herself yelling. "I'm on my own here. It's the entire freaking island against me. I don't want to stay here for a month. I don't want to stay here for a day. I just want my life to be normal again."

Nikos stepped back, frowning. "I'm really sorry you feel that way," he said. He was quiet for a moment before he continued. "Let me know when you want to start the work again. I'll be here to help."

"Really?" Anna asked.

"Of course," he replied. "Wouldn't want you having to stick around any longer than necessary." He turned around and left, shutting the door hard behind him.

Anna felt a tear hit her chest, and she brought her hands to her eyes to wipe them. She slumped down on the bed, pushing her computer to the side so she could crawl under the covers.

Make that zero people who would give her the time of day. She could try to salvage things with Nikos, but did she even want to?

Of course I do, she thought, instantly cross with herself at her hash words to him. He had made her first few days on the island far more enjoyable than they would have been otherwise, and he had been so generous to help her. But there was no denying that she was attracted to him. And after what had happened with his cousin Elena earlier, it was probably a good thing not to be spending all her time with a cute townie. Summer flings were for summer vacations, and this was no vacation. She had work to do.

But for the moment, Anna couldn't bring herself to do anything but lie in her bed and sob. This was going to be a long month.

"**B**ullshit!" Lizzy shouted over the phone. "I don't buy that for a second."

"I don't care if you believe it," the lawyer said. "It's true." Sofia Kafatos sat across from Anna at the table in the summer house. She was the first person on the island Anna had seen in a suit.

"You're telling me that dump is over the twenty-thousand-euro tax threshold?"

Anna winced slightly at hearing her sister call the summer house a dump, but she couldn't disagree, either.

"It probably is," she said.

"Even without a separate entrance?" Anna asked.

"This is a nice plot of land," Sofia said. "It would be easy enough for the next buyer to construct a drive to connect with the road. It may not be in great condition, but the property itself is likely worth at least eighty thousand euros. If you were in a more touristy area or on the other side of the hills, it would be worth twice as much, even in its current condition. Though it will need its own driveway and be independent of the main house's utilities before it hits the market."

Anna heard Lizzy sigh on the other end of the line, but with the poor connection it just sounded like static.

"Remember though," Sofia said, "you don't pay tax on the first twenty thousand, even if it's over the threshold. Then it's five per cent on the next forty, and ten per cent on the next hundred and sixty. So, if it were worth eighty thousand, which I'm not saying it is because I'm not qualified to value it, then you'd only pay four thousand euros in tax, and you have a year to pay it since you are foreign nationals. But if you suspect the value of the property will go up before you sell, you should pay now. Any other valuation may mean your tax bill goes up, too."

Anna closed her eyes and rolled her shoulders back. All these numbers and deadlines were making her head spin. She had no idea what the right thing to do was, or if she was even being given an option at this point.

Lizzy cleared her throat. "Sofia?" she asked, and the lawyer leaned forward. "Is it still possible to turn down the inheritance?"

"*What?*" Anna shouted. "After everything I've gone through to get it for us?"

Sofia held up a hand. "Your father's will was verified just over three months ago. So, you still technically have a couple of weeks before you have to claim anything."

Anna shook her head. As if she could see it, Lizzy replied. "Banana, we will talk about this later. Sofia, I think we're done for today. We'll call you when we've made a decision."

"Of course," Sofia said, gathering her things. She looked at Anna. "You know where to find me."

As Sofia left, Anna picked up the phone and took it off speaker. "What the hell was that about?" she asked. "I've flown all the way out here and spent over a thousand dollars on home-improvement goods, and you're thinking you might not want it anymore?" Anna had considered taking Christos's offer to help pay for things, but it hadn't felt right, so she had practically drained her account, assuming it would be overflowing soon once the house sold. She wasn't left with much.

"Two thousand euros is a lot of money, Banana. We don't have that right now."

"Oh, but you were fine with me spending half my savings on a plane ticket and home repairs? Yeah, right! That money is all I have right now, too."

"At least you have a job that pays you!"

Anna sighed. She didn't reply. She knew she should tell Lizzy about Marcus. About her job. About everything. But she couldn't bring herself to say it. She wasn't even sure she knew how to.

It turned out she didn't need to.

"You lost your job, didn't you, Banana?"

Again, Anna didn't reply.

"Does this have to do with Marcus?"

More silence.

"Fine, Anna, don't answer me." It was jarring to hear Lizzy call her anything other than Banana. "But know this. I wouldn't be saying this if it weren't desperately true. Martin and I just can't afford two grand right now. We have a lot going on. If you want to pay for it and then claim it back from me after the sale, fine. If you want to give up the inheritance, fine. If you want me to sign the whole thing over to you and leave you alone, fine. I'll do what you want. But we just don't have the money."

Anna began to cry. She had been doing a lot of that in the last week. "Lizzy, what am I supposed to do? Tell me what the right choice is."

"I can't do that," she said. "It's your money. It's your decision."

The two were quiet for a long time, Lizzy's breathing the only indication she was still there. They had always been good at that – sitting in silence to let each other process. It was several minutes before Lizzy broke that silence.

"Banana, I have to go. Let me know what you decide."

"Love y—" Anna started, but the line was dead.

Anna woke to a knock on the door. She had lain on her bed after hanging up with Lizzy, confused and emotionally exhausted. She must have fallen asleep.

Putting her feet on the floor, she shuffled over toward the door, but as she reached a couple of feet in front of the entrance, she felt a sharp, searing pain shoot through her toe and into her foot. She screamed and fell to the floor, clutching her leg close to her chest.

The door burst open, and Elena came in, long hair flying. "What the hell happened?" she asked, holding her hand under Anna's foot, which was now dripping with blood.

"It must be a shard from when Nikos stepped on a bowl," she said through clenched teeth.

"Nah, that's Jewish weddings I think," Elena said. "The Greeks are plates. And we don't really do that anymore."

"Huh?" Anna asked, unable to understand anything but the fact that her toe was now throbbing.

"Never mind," Elena said, running to the kitchen and returning with a clean, damp cloth. "You'll have to tell me the story later. For now, let's get you healed up." She reached into her purse and pulled out a makeup bag. After some rummaging, she found a pair of tweezers. She took the cloth and dabbed at Anna's toe, which made her wince from the pain.

"Sorry," Elena said. "I'll be as quick as I can." Then she put the tweezers close to Anna's toe, pinched them, and pulled. Anna screamed as a half-inch shard came out of her toe. Elena wrapped her foot in the cloth and squeezed. The pressure helped the pain subside a bit.

Elena held the tweezers up close to Anna's face so she could see.

"I felt the whole thing," Anna said. "I really don't need to see it."

"Oh, please," Elena responded, "I've had eyebrow hairs tougher than this guy." Then she smiled.

"Let's get you to the table," she added, offering Anna a hand. Anna accepted, and Elena pulled her up on her good foot and held onto her as she hopped the few feet to the table. Anna pulled out a chair and sat down.

"I'll be back," Elena said and, as quickly as she had appeared, was gone.

Anna's phone was on the table, so she picked it up. It was nearly ten at night. She had napped for almost eight hours. That probably didn't even qualify as a nap anymore, just a normal sleep.

She unlocked the phone so she could sneak in one more Instagram session on her remaining data, but she must have left it switched on because she had a notification saying she had used it all up. She connected to the WiFi instead.

For the first time, Anna wondered what was happening with the utilities. The property was legally separate from Christos and Eirini's, but clearly they were still paying for utilities, as the lights and water still worked. She considered hoping they wouldn't notice but quickly decided that probably wouldn't work very well in the long run. She would have to start buttering them up for now so they wouldn't leave her in the dark.

At that moment, Elena stormed back in through the door with a first aid kit tucked under one arm. She knelt down in front of Anna and unwrapped the cloth from her foot, examining the wound.

"I'm sure you didn't come here to wrap up my yet-to-be-injured foot," Anna said. "Did you need something, or were you just coming to say hi?"

"Nikos told me what happened yesterday," Elena said as she dug through the kit. "What you said. I wanted to talk to you about it."

Anna shrugged her shoulders. "I was upset, but I wasn't wrong."

Elena stopped tending to her foot and looked up at her. "But, see, that's it. You are wrong. It's not the entire island against you. Nikos has been bending over backward trying to make sure you know that you have a friend here." She looked back down as she squirted antiseptic onto a pad and dabbed it on Anna's toe.

Anna winced as the alcohol made contact with the wound, stinging her toe. She fought the urge to twitch her foot; she didn't want to kick Elena in the face while she was trying to help her. She didn't need to piss off another of her allies.

"I'm sorry I said that, but it sure feels like I'm alone in this. I have to make this massive decision all on my own. And Nikos would influence that decision."

Elena raised her eyebrows. "Oh yeah? You crushing on my cousin?"

Anna rolled her eyes. "Not like that necessarily. I just mean that he was so close with Giorgos, and he works for

Christos. It doesn't really seem like he would be that objective." And, yes, I'm crushing on your cousin, and it makes it harder to be objective.

"Sure," Elena said, pursing her lips as she wrapped a bandage around the now-covered wound and the rest of Anna's foot. "There, all done. Let's see how it feels to walk on it."

She helped Anna stand up and then motioned for her to take a step forward. The wound was in her third toe, so it didn't carry much weight. She could walk relatively normally.

"Thank you," Anna said. "I'm not sure what I would have done if that had happened without you here."

"To be fair, it probably wouldn't have happened today if I hadn't knocked on the door."

Anna laughed. "Still, better than it happening with me on my own. I'm not great with blood, especially my own. You, on the other hand, were on it."

"Yeah, well, my mother was a nurse," Elena said. "She sort of drilled it into me to be prepared for stuff like this."

Anna sat down on the bed and hugged a pillow to her chest. Elena sat down next to her, placing a hand on her knee.

"You know, why don't I help you with this decision?" Elena said. "I'm definitely honest, and I didn't know your dad that well. Plus, I inherited my mom's place when she died, so I know a little about this stuff."

Elena had a matter-of-fact look on her face that made

Anna feel she could trust her to be objective. Maybe it would be nice to talk it through with someone.

"Well, the issue is that my sister can't afford to help pay the tax on it. But we have to pay the tax before I do all the work, or the amount we have to pay will go up, and I won't get the money back that I've already spent on getting here and buying new stuff."

Elena nodded her head as Anna spoke. "Why are you fixing it up instead of just putting it on the market as is? I know you wouldn't get as much for it, but you could still sell it, I'm sure."

"I don't know," Anna said. "But if I'm going to be here until it sells, I don't want to live like this. Plus, I looked it up, and if I fixed it up, I could more than double my investment."

"And you don't have the money to pay for it yourself?"

"Well," Anna replied, "technically I do, but it would mean using the rest of my savings, which would mean I would have to use the money from the sale to be able to afford a plane ticket home. Which is fine, since I don't have a job anymore, but my last pay check comes through this week, and I'd have to live on that until I left. And since it's not even enough to get me home, I don't know how realistic that is."

Elena nodded some more, considering what Anna was saying.

"Or," Anna continued, "I could leave on my flight in two days and refuse the inheritance, and the house would go to Christos and Eirini."

"But you don't want to do that?"

Anna paused a moment before responding, but she already knew the answer. "No, I don't. I've flown all the way out here, I've invested a lot already in fixing it up, and I think it's only fair that we get the money from the house after everything Giorgos put us through."

"Okay," Elena said, paying no notice to her comment about Giorgos. She seemed to be holding up her promise to be objective. "I think you should do it."

"Really?"

"Yeah. Of course. It's what you want, and it makes sense. And we can do it."

"*We?*"

"Yes, of course *we*. Nikos and I will help you with the house. Between Christos and me, I promise you won't go hungry. And then you get to take it one step at a time."

Anna took a deep breath. Maybe she *could* do this. "I don't know," she said. "My head is still sort of spinning. And there's still the matter of the whole island being against me, even if you two are helping. And that's assuming Nikos will get over what I said."

"Well, that's just a little dramatic. We're all adults, and people will learn to live with your decision. Life goes on. But why don't you sleep on it? I'll come over in the morning with some coffee. It's my day off, so we can spend the morning crunching some numbers and figuring this thing out. I can even change your bandage."

Anna nodded. Despite her sleep, she still felt pretty tired.

These last few days must have really taken it out of her, she realised, what with the physical labor of getting everything for the renovations and the emotional labor of the decision she had to make. More rest would be good.

"I'll see you tomorrow then," Elena said, squeezing Anna's knee and getting up.

"Yes, see you then," Anna replied with a wave as Elena walked out the door. She saw that Elena had left her first aid kit on the table, probably in case anything went wrong in the night. At least she'd be back in the morning.

A few minutes later, Anna hobbled over to the kitchen to grab a pre-bedtime snack, deciding to take the whole tray of pastries with her so she wouldn't have to get up again. As she sat on her bed eating a piece of *bougatsa* and opened her laptop, she wondered if it was possible to be in love with a dessert. She might end up deciding to stay in Santorini just for the food alone. She leaned carefully over the tray as she ate so she wouldn't get drops of custard or flakes of filo on the new sheets.

Licking her fingers, she scrolled through some Manhattan job listings she had pulled up on. Annoyingly, it seemed that all she was qualified to do after spending a whole year as a gallery assistant was... be a gallery assistant. And she didn't want to do that anymore.

Anna looked over at her camera, which she had unpacked and put on the bookshelf by the door. She would have to take it out at some point; the island was too beautiful for her not to take photos. But, for now, she just stared at it.

She hadn't taken a single photo since she had started at the gallery. She had thought about it occasionally, wondering why she didn't just go out one weekend and shoot. She always chalked it up to being around so much talent at the gallery that she felt intimidated. But now she realized that it had been because of Marcus. She hadn't wanted him to ever feel like she was using him or her position to try to become a photographer, even if that's what she would have wanted.

Now she wondered if she should have taken more advantage of her situation. She'd spent so much time caring about what he would think – working harder than anyone during the day, and being as passive and inoffensive as possible when she was with him at night – when she could see clearly now that he had never spared such a thought for her.

On a whim, Anna typed, "MarMac Emerging Talent contest" into the search bar. She clicked over to the website and read through the rules. The deadline was eleven days away, but she was only ten days away from not being an employee anymore. The terms said nothing about former employees or anyone with a relationship with Marcus. So Anna downloaded the form and filled it out, dating it the one day that it would be valid. She uploaded it to an email along with the images she had taken for her Forgotten Manhattan Landmarks series.

And then she set the email to send on June 8, just eleven days away.

Anna let out a deep breath. If she was going to be dragged halfway around the world to deal with her deadbeat dad's estate and get fired from her job because of it, she sure as hell wasn't going to hold herself back anymore. She had enough other things doing that for her already. Maybe when she sold the house she could use the money to finally do what she wanted to do.

Anna got back out of bed, walked over to the bookshelf and grabbed her camera. Miraculously, the battery wasn't dead, so she scrolled through some of her old photos. Maybe she was biased, but she thought they were pretty good. She also thought she could do better now. She pulled out the memory card, went back over to her bed, plugged it into her laptop and began editing.

She ended up editing photos all night, from vacations on Cape Cod to shots from her high school reunion a couple of years prior. She made new presets, edited out tourists, and even tried some photo manipulation techniques. What felt like a few minutes later, the sun came up and filtered through the windows at the front of the house as Anna finally crawled under the covers and drifted off to sleep.

"So, any progress on your decision?" Elena asked, sipping her coffee. Anna had only slept a couple of hours, but she felt more energetic than she had in a long time.

"Actually, yes," Anna replied. "I want to do it. Lizzy said I could have the house myself since she can't afford the tax payment, and I think I could fix it up enough to give me enough money to live off for a while so I can pursue my dreams for once." She smiled as she took the lid off the coffee Elena had brought her, blew across the top and took a sip.

"Well, well," Elena responded, smiling, "look at you all confident and sure of yourself. What brought that on?"

Anna considered her response for a moment. "I'm just tired of letting things happen *to* me. I want to make things happen *for* me instead."

Nodding, Elena smiled again. "And what are these dreams you want to pursue?"

"Well..." Anna said, spinning the computer round to show Elena some of her edits from the night before, "I want to be a photographer. I always have."

Elena gasped and pulled the computer closer to her, clicking through the photos one by one. "Anna, these are wonderful," she said. "I can't believe you took these."

"Thanks," Anna said, sitting back and smiling, too. "There's a lot of editing on there."

"Yeah, but you did that, too," Elena said, clicking quickly through the photos. She clasped her hands together and looked up at Anna. "Oh my god, you have to take photos of me!"

Anna laughed. "What? Why?"

"For my Instagram!" Elena said. "I'm trying to get enough followers so that I can start getting free stuff."

Anna remembered what Nikos had said about influencers before and laughed again. "What sort of pictures do you want?"

"I don't know," Elena replied, shrugging. "Lots of different kinds. Some posed, some while we're out, stuff like that. Basically, if you could be my personal paparazzi, that would be great."

They both giggled now, but Anna didn't think it was a terrible idea. It would give her something to do and help make sure she could get out of the house with someone other than Nikos.

"I would be honored to be your paparazzi," she said. They clinked their paper coffee cups together. "But, in the meantime, I need to get a valuation booked. Any thoughts on that?"

"Mmm, yes," Elena said. "A friend of the family did it for me when I inherited my mother's house. I can make sure he gives you a good price."

"That would be amazing," Anna said, looking over the to-do list she had made in her manic night of productivity. There were some things on there that were probably unnecessary – the summer house probably didn't need a pool, and she wasn't sure what "Moroccan pattern" referred to – but some things, like the valuation and utilities, needed to be addressed sooner rather than later.

Elena looked over at the list, and her eyes went wide. "Wow, we really have our work cut out for us," she said.

"Yeah, but we have a while to worry about most of this," Anna responded. "It's the tax-related stuff we need to do more quickly."

"No problem," Elena said, pulling out her phone. "I'll text Vasilios now."

Anna ran through the list, scratching out the unnecessary additions and adding up the others. She had already spent over a thousand dollars on things for the house. The tax bill would drain the rest of her savings, and her pay check would barely be enough for the essential items on her list.

"I think I'm going to need a job," she said with a sigh.

"How good are you at waiting tables?" Elena asked without looking up from her phone. Anna looked up at her. "Why?"

"The cafe at the resort always needs more people during the summer. It's about to be peak tourist season, and we're always understaffed, but good local people are hard to find for seasonal work. I'm sure Xenia would give you some shifts if you asked."

"Well, I'm not exactly a local. But do you think she would pay under the table?" Anna asked. "I don't know if I can get a job on a tourist visa."

Elena reached into her bag and took out a wad of cash, grinning as she held it up to Anna. "I can say definitively that she will."

8

Anna's first day at the cafe was both the easiest and hardest first workday of Anna's life.

It was the easiest because it turns out that waiting tables at a beach cafe isn't that difficult. The menu was in English, at least.

It was hard because her feet had never hurt so badly in her life, and there was something sticky all over her running shoes. Not that she had been doing much running in the two weeks since she'd arrived; the hills were exercise enough. But it was a shame to see them covered in cocktail syrups and whatever else was on the floor.

The thing heaviest on Anna's mind was how much more satisfied she felt after one day's work at the cafe than she ever had after working at the gallery. What she was doing here was no more important, but it at least felt productive. She felt useful.

Anna was mopping the floor at the end of her shift when Nikos walked in, clearly at the end of his shift as well. All of his clothes were covered in paint and drywall, including the very holey tee shirt he was wearing. If Anna looked close enough, she could see his abs peeking through one of the larger holes.

She started blushing when she realized she was looking closely enough to see them. She turned around and kept mopping, waving over her shoulder as he walked past and sat down at the bar. Elena took his order and gave it to the kitchen, then said she was going to grab more napkins from the storeroom.

"We still alright to run to the store?" Anna asked Nikos, trying to smile as if nothing was wrong. They were meant to go buy more supplies that evening.

Things had improved between the two of them over the last week, but this was the first time they had been alone together since the argument. He had come over once, but that was with Elena when their friend had come to value the house. For someone unqualified to give an estimate, Sofia had been pretty spot-on with hers. The four thousand euros – or nearly forty-five hundred dollars – was out of Anna's account as soon as possible so that she could start on the rest of the list.

"Yeah, no problem," Nikos said as the chef put his food down in front of him. "You have your list?"

Anna pulled a slightly damp sheet of paper out of the back pocket of her shorts. Thankfully, it was still legible. "Yep, just windows and paint."

"Did you pick out a color yet?"

Anna sighed. "Not quite," she said, showing Nikos the

three samples stapled to her list. "I like all of them so much." She set the mop aside and sat down next to Nikos. Elena's promise that Tuesdays were slow was an understatement; there was no one else in the cafe.

Nikos took the paper from Anna's hand, brushing his fingers against hers, but he didn't look up and wink. He just looked at the samples. There was a trendy emerald green, a lilac grey, and a deep, shocking blue.

"I like the green," he said, "but I think it's too dark. It's a small little space, and this would make it feel *too* small."

Anna nodded her head. "Yeah, that makes sense."

"The grey looks like what we're using in the hotel rooms," he said, searching for a similar-colored splatter on his shirt and holding it up next to the sample. They both laughed.

"Yeah, that's actually where I got the idea from. I like it too, but isn't it a bit boring?"

"I don't know," Nikos answered, "I like it. Plus, the blue is going to give you a similar problem to the green. You could always buy some decorations in blue."

Anna nodded again. "Yeah, I like that."

She paused for a moment before continuing, considering if it was worth saying anything. But if they were going to be spending time together again, she wanted to clear the air.

"Listen, Nikos, about last week—"

"No," he interrupted, "don't even mention it. I understand where you were coming from."

"I have to," she said. "I owe you an apology. Elena was right; you were doing so much to help me, and I basically told you it meant nothing. I'm so sorry."

"Thanks," Nikos said, smiling. "Elena needs to mind her own business, but I do appreciate it. I don't want you to feel like you're alone in this. Giorgos left you his house for a reason, and that doesn't make you a villain. At least, I have yet to notice a twirly mustache."

Anna laughed. "Just wait until you catch me on an off day." Nikos held her gaze, and she started to blush again. It seemed things were truly back to normal, as confusing as that may be.

"You two kiss and make up?" Elena asked as she walked in with a pack of napkins tucked under her arm.

"What?" Anna asked, jumping up and grabbing the mop. "Of course not."

Nikos laughed. "Yes, Anna apologized for being the worst person in the world and admitted to having a mustache."

"Of course," Elena said. "Makes perfect sense. Now, shall we close up and get out of here?"

A few hours later, Anna walked up to the summer house with a can of paint in each hand to find Eirini waiting at the door.

"Hello Anna," she said, somewhat formally. But then again, that was fitting given that she had only seen her twice since the drive up from the resort that first day on the island. Anna had bumped into Christos a few times, but Eirini had stayed firmly out of sight for the last two weeks.

"Hi Eirini," Anna replied, the handles of the paint cans digging into her fingers. She adjusted them subtly, not wanting Eirini to feel she was trying to send a message but also unsure of how long she'd be standing there.

"Your grandfather would like to invite you to dinner at our house tomorrow."

Anna noticed that Eirini had excluded herself from the invitation, but she recognized an olive branch when she saw one, and she knew she would need their help if she was going to get the house on the market in the time frame she wanted to, so she took it.

"Yes, of course. I'd love to. What time should I come over?"

"You may come inside at nine pm. Please don't be late." And with that she walked past Anna and back into the main house.

"What was that?" Elena asked, coming up behind her with the rollers and trays.

"I've just been invited to dinner, it seems." Anna set one of the paint cans down to open the door. "Tomorrow night."

"That's great," Elena replied. "Maybe you and your grandparents can get on speaking terms."

"Well, I'll have to at some point. I have to talk to them about the utilities."

"Maybe don't bring that up at your dinner, yeah? Give them some time."

"Yeah, yeah, fine." Anna set the paint down on the table as she came in. "But it has to happen at some point."

"What has to happen at some point?" Nikos asked, strolling through the door with a glass panel in his hands, but Anna didn't answer him. She was too busy staring at his abs again. And she didn't have to look through the holes in his shirt this time.

"There is literally no reason for you to be shirtless right now," Elena said, rolling her eyes.

"Oh, come on, that's not fair. The corner of the window-pane got caught in one the holes of my shirt, so I figured it would be better to just take it off."

"Sure," Elena said, glaring at him as she walked past. "I'm going to get the rest of the bags. When I come back in, you'd better have the same amount of clothing on that you do right now, or more." Anna chuckled, and Elena spun round and pointed at her. "That goes for you, too." She held two fingers up to her eyes and then pointed them at Anna and Nikos as she backed out, closing the door behind her.

"Flimsy excuse," Anna said, unwrapping the things on the table.

"Oh, I'm sorry." Nikos leaned the windowpane against the wall where it would be installed and then walked over next to her. "I was under the impression that you were checking out the merchandise earlier. Was I wrong? Am I making you uncomfortable?"

"Was not," Anna said, but she knew her face was giving her away.

98

Nikos inched closer, and Anna could feel the heat coming off him.

"Ew, you're all sweaty!" she said, pushing him away gently, her hands running across his stomach as she did so. She felt a spark run through her, as if he had shocked her. It had been a while since she'd felt so flustered over a guy, probably since her first night with Marcus. Even then, it had been more about her being impressed with Marcus's status. What she was feeling now was pure, unadulterated attraction.

"Yeah, well, you are, too," he said, but he backed away. Anna was grateful. As nice as it was to be back on speaking – and joking – terms with Nikos, she didn't need the added complication of a romantic relationship. Though she did find him pretty irresistible...

"Who wants the caulk?" Elena shouted as she walked back through the door, and Anna startled before she realized what she meant. She turned around to look just in time to see a bottle of window sealant flying at her and barely managed to catch it.

"Glad to see no further clothing has been removed," Elena said. "Now, let's install some windows, shall we?"

That evening, Anna sat in the bathtub, fully clothed, staring out the new bathroom window at the view over the town while holding the phone up to her ear. You couldn't see the sunset from this side of the island, but the sky still lit up all kinds of beautiful colors.

"I just don't understand why you have to speak to that vile woman at all," her mother Grace said, the sound of silverware clinking against plates in the background.

"She's living on *her* property," Lizzy said. "She's using *her* WiFi to talk to us right now."

"Technically it's Anna's property," Grace said.

"Mom has a point," Anna added from the tub. "But so do you, Lizzy. I'm in her backyard. I have to play nice if I want to be able to live here in peace. They've made it so much easier for me, letting me use their utilities and Christos letting Nikos drive me around in the truck."

"Ooh, Nikos!" Lizzy teased. "Isn't he handsome? I knew you two would hit it off."

"He's nice," Anna said. "He and his cousin Elena are the only friends I have here, and they've been really good to me."

"Friends, sure." From her tone, Anna could imagine a sly grin on Lizzy's face.

"Take my advice and stay far away from Greek men," Grace said, the slurp of what Anna was certain was a cocktail sounding in her ear. "Nothing good can come from it."

"Except, I don't know, two beautiful children?" Lizzy said, but Grace was now talking to someone in the background.

"Mom? You there?" Anna asked.

"Oh, sorry dears, I have to go. Try not to die in Greece, Anna; it would undo all of the hard work I've put in over the years to keep you away from that place." And then the background noise stopped. It was just Anna and Lizzy left on the call.

"Well, isn't she just a ray of sunshine, as usual."

"Thank you for talking to her with me," Anna said. "I couldn't have faced her without you." Despite being the only parent she knew, Anna had never seen eye to eye with her mother, especially not about important things, and since leaving home Anna had made it a point to always have Lizzy by her side when delivering big news.

"Any time, Banana."

There were a few moments of silence before Anna continued.

"Liz, I'm so sorry about the last time we talked. I was just stressed out, and it's not your fault."

"Don't be silly," she said. "You had every right to be frustrated. I forced you out there and then left you hanging."

"Well, it might not have been such a bad thing," Anna said. "That job was toxic, and I've never been much of a city girl."

"You starting to like it out there?"

"It doesn't suck," Anna admitted. "At least not for the summer. Though, I'll be glad to take an actual shower when I get home. There's only a bath at the summer house."

"Yeah, I remember," Lizzy said. "There's a really nice one in the main house."

"Yeah, well, I don't think I'm going to be showering there anytime soon." Anna sighed, feeling the heat of the evening air and longing for a cold shower. "You've never told me much about the time you spent here for the funeral last year."

"Only because you never let me."

"Now that's not true."

"Oh, it absolutely is," Lizzy said. "I was brimming with excitement when I got back, but every time I tried to tell you about it, you just asked me again why I went. So I stopped trying. I know it was weird for you, that you didn't think he deserved our grief – Mom's line, by the way – but all I wanted was to talk to you about it and you shut me down."

"Okay," Anna said, "then tell me now."

"What it was like, or why I went?"

Anna paused. "Both."

For a moment, things were silent, and Anna knew Lizzy was thinking. She could picture her with her head tilted to the right and her brows pressed together – her thinking face since she was a kid.

"Well, I went because on some level I didn't quite believe Mom's side of things."

"Why not?"

"I don't know," Lizzy said. "It just didn't sit right with me. I'd had Dad for ten years, and I was old enough to know that there was more going on than she told us at the time. I asked again a few years back, when she should have felt able to tell me the whole truth, but it was the same lines she gave us back then. So, I was suspicious."

"Did you figure out what she was lying about?"

"No, not until I went. Let's just say that the people of Santorini have a very different view of what happened between Mom and Dad."

"Well, of course they do," Anna said. "They were *his* friends. *His* family. They had to take his side."

"I don't know, Banana. I think there was more going on."

Anna shook her head. Conspiracy theories about their parents' past wouldn't do them any good now. "Okay, so what was it like when you came here?"

"Well, it was beautiful, but you already know that. And the people were so kind to me."

"And you met Nikos?"

"I met Nikos," Lizzy said, and again Anna could hear the smile on her face. "He was so sweet. He and Dad clearly loved each other."

"Yeah, it seems like they were really close."

"I think he put all the love and attention into Nikos that he didn't get to put into us. Did you know he sent him to college in England so he could study at the London School of Economics?"

"*What?*" This was definitely news to Anna. "Why does he still work for Christos then?"

"Well, he tried to drop out when his aunt died, but Dad wouldn't let him. He took care of Elena while Nikos was away. Just after he graduated, Dad had his first heart attack, so Nikos came back to take his job. I guess he never left."

Anna sat with her mouth wide open, processing this information. The Giorgos Lizzy was describing sounded so much more like the man Anna had remembered from when she was a child, but she had buried those memories. Her mother had told her not to trust him, so she didn't trust her memories of him, either.

"How did you find all of this out?"

"Greek people are very chatty after a few glasses of ouzo."

Anna made a face. Elena had forced her to try some of the licorice-tasting alcohol at work, and it made her feel sick just to think about it.

"Nikos is a good guy, Banana," Lizzy said.

"I know he is. I just don't have time for anything but friends right now."

Lizzy sighed. "If you say so. I'm just saying, if I hadn't been married already, my trip might have been a very different one."

"You were here for Giorgos's funeral!"

Lizzy laughed. "I know. I'm kidding. Sort of. But the point remains. He's a catch."

Anna nodded her head, even though she knew Lizzy couldn't see her. The truth was that he *was* a catch, and Anna knew it. He was kind and funny and smart, not to mention insanely good-looking. That much had been obvious from the moment she'd spotted him in the airport.

But he also wasn't *too* nice, as that first encounter had also proven. And Anna was, annoyingly, to everyone including herself, the type of girl who turned up her nose at "nice guys." Marcus certainly wasn't a nice guy. Nikos was, but it didn't feel performative like it did with so many of the "nice guys" she had met in Manhattan. It was just a genuine part of who he was, right alongside the snarkiness and impatience. It made him pretty damn irresistible.

"Anyway," Lizzy continued, "you know as well as anyone how great he is. But if you don't want to go there, at least get to know him so you can learn more about Dad. I think you'll find there's a lot more than Grace Linton would lead you to believe."

9

Anna gripped a tray of baklava leftover from work in one hand and raised the other to knock on her grandparents' door. She hadn't been sure which door she should use for dinner, so she'd played it safe and gone through her gate and through the grass to the front door.

A moment later, Eirini answered the door, her breathing shallow and her apron covered in spots of juice and grease.

"Why are you at the front door?" she asked. "Come in, come in." She ushered Anna through to the front room of the house.

The second Anna stepped through the door, she noticed how much cooler it was inside. Her summer house may have air conditioning, but Eirini and Christos's home seemed to be more like a naturally insulated cave. The walls were bright white and smooth, curving like rock above her to create a dome over the lounge she now stood in.

She slipped off her shoes and followed Eirini through

the room. Four other, smaller, chamber-like rooms opened off the back of the lounge. The door to the far left one was open, and Anna could see Christos slicing some pita on a table in the middle of a kitchen. Sunlight was shining in on him from the left, and Anna realized the kitchen must contain the other door to the courtyard.

Eirini waved Anna through to the kitchen and beckoned for her to sit. Anna held out the baklava. "I brought this from work."

Eirini nodded, took the tray from her hands, and set it on the counter behind her.

"Anna!" Christos exclaimed, putting down the bread knife and coming over, arms outstretched. Anna gave him a big, wordless hug. They may not be able to understand each other well, but Anna knew what she was feeling now. Gratitude. And a little bit of sweat from Christos's brow, but that was alright.

"It smells amazing in here," Anna said as Christos pulled away, getting a whiff of something herbal. "What's for dinner?"

"Traditional Santorini food," Eirini said, wiping her hands on her apron and lifting the lid of a pot on the stove, stirring the contents a few times before re-covering it. She then prodded some meatballs frying in a pan and said something over her shoulder in Greek to Christos, who left Anna's side to grab three bowls, three plates, three cups and three wine glasses from the shelves, placing them carefully on the table. He then retrieved cutlery and some blue-and-white-checked cloth napkins from a drawer next to the sink, laying them out as well.

By the time he'd finished, Eirini was turning the heat off on the stove and pulling what looked like a casserole out of the oven, her apron the only barrier between her hand and the presumably boiling hot pan. She set it down on a potholder in the middle of the table, the creamy, cheesy topping still bubbling. It looked like enough to feed generous portions to ten people. A few moments later, a plate of fried discs of some sort joined the setup, along with a bowl of what could best be described as yellow mush topped with red onions and capers. Last came a bowl full of the meatballs and a bottle of wine.

"*Moussaka*," she said, pointing to the casserole, followed by, "meatballs, tomatoes, beans." Apparently the yellow mush was some kind of bean, then.

"Wine?" Christos added, holding up the bottle and smiling at Anna. She smiled back and nodded in response.

The three of them sat at the set places, Anna at the head of the table between them at her grandfather's insistence. Christos then began making everyone's plates. He slapped a massive portion of *moussaka* on Anna's, along with half a dozen meatballs, three fried tomatoes, and nearly a cup of the bean mush. She gulped silently as she wondered how she was going to eat even half of it. She wished she knew more about whether it was rude in Greece to leave food on your plate. She hoped not.

She needn't have worried. The food was so delicious

that she ended up devouring it before she even realized she had. The *moussaka* was creamy and rich, the tomato fritters tasted fresh and herbal, the meatballs were juicy... even the bean mush was incredible. It tasted of lemon and garlic and salt. She barely said a word the entire meal as she was so busy eating, simply nodding when her grandparents asked about her plans to fix up the house. She mopped up all the remnants on her plate with a pita until it looked freshly cleaned.

"Eirini, that was amazing," she said to her grandmother, and for the first time she saw a hint of a smile.

"I am glad you liked it," she said. "These are all traditional recipes from here on the island, and I wasn't sure how much of it you would be getting on your own or at the cafe. We all know Nikos isn't feeding you this sort of food."

Eirini rolled her eyes, and Anna grinned as she remembered how her first two meals in Greece had been from McDonald's. It definitely paled in comparison to the smorgasbord she had just experienced.

"Well, now I'll know what to ask for," she said.

Eirini and Christos muttered to each other across the table in Greek for a few moments before Christos shrugged and Eirini turned to Anna.

"Anna, we heard that you accepted the inheritance," she said, "and that you're fixing up the house. Is that true?"

Anna was surprised; she had just assumed that Eirini and Christos would be kept in the loop. Now she had to worry about them being upset not only because she was selling the house but also because she hadn't told them what she'd decided.

"Yes, it is," she said, "and I'm so sorry I didn't tell you. I assumed the lawyers would tell you."

She braced herself for a negative reaction, but none came. Instead, Eirini smiled broadly at Christos and then at her.

"We are so glad to hear that," she said.

Anna couldn't believe what she was hearing. "You are?"

"Of course," she said. "We're so looking forward to you spending more time here. It was always our greatest disappointment that we didn't know you and your sister better."

"Well, I'm looking forward to spending time here, too," Anna said, smiling to herself. "I'm really enjoying seeing more of the island. Nikos and Elena are taking me to Oia next week."

"Ah, Oia!" Christos repeated, and Anna suspected he was understanding more of the conversation than she had originally thought.

"Do you have everything you need for the summer house?" Eirini asked. "Can we do anything to help fix it up?"

Anna paused for a moment. Elena had told her not to bring up the utilities, but that was when they thought Eirini and Christos would be angry. Now that they were offering, it could be good to discuss.

"Actually," she said, "there is something I could use your help with."

"Anything."

"The utilities are currently all run through your house. Nikos has spoken with some people who can help split them, and I'll obviously pay for everything, but we'll need to access your property in order to do that."

Eirini waved her hand dismissively. "Don't be silly, you can keep them together. You'll use so little that we probably won't notice. You can always just chip in on the months you spend here."

Anna frowned. "Yes, but what about when I leave?"

"Then you won't be using much water and electricity, will you?" Eirini laughed, as if the suggestion was ridiculous, and that's when Anna realized what was happening. Eirini thought that she was fixing the house up for herself. She still didn't understand that Anna planned to sell it. It was the last thing she wanted to bring up now, but she had started it. She had to set things straight.

"That's very generous of you, but in order to put the house on the market, I'll have to split the utilities and add a driveway."

As Anna's words sank in, Eirini's smile got smaller and smaller, before slipping from her face entirely.

"You are going to sell the house?" she asked quietly through pursed lips.

Anna nodded. "That's the plan."

Eirini and Christos began speaking in Greek again, this time louder and more quickly. Even without understanding their words, Anna could tell that Christos was trying to calm Eirini down, but she was getting more and more worked up, standing up from the table and pacing back and forth across the kitchen. Raising her voice, she started speaking English again.

"You Linton women, coming in and taking everything we have. First, you take our son away, and when he comes back years later, he's a completely different person. Then he dies, and you can't take him away anymore, so you come for his home, the only thing we have left of him."

Anna sat pressed against the back of her chair, incredulous. She knew her grandparents blamed her mother for things; that much had been clear. But now they were blaming the entire Linton family, including their own grandchildren.

"I don't think that's entirely fair," she said, a feeble attempt at defending herself.

"No, it's not," Eirini said, sighing. "But neither is the fact that my son is gone, and now his daughter has come along to halve the value of our home and erase every trace of him from our lives. So if you'll excuse me, I don't really care about fair right now."

Anna sighed before raising her voice slightly to match Eirini's pitch. "I'm sorry you feel that way. I didn't ask for this house, though. He saw fit to leave it to me and my sister. So as far as I'm concerned, what I choose to do with *my* house is up to *me*. I'm really sorry that it's an inconvenience, but after all *your son* put us through, I think we deserve to get something out of it."

Several seconds passed. Eirini looked at Christos, who appeared shell-shocked. She looked at Anna and frowned. And then she spoke again.

"Your father told me once that he wasn't sure what your mother had told you about him, but that it must have been terrible for you to never reach out. He lived in the hope that you would one day, but he never blamed you when you didn't. Not after what he imagined your mother made up. Of course, if you can believe his own parents, none of it is true."

Anna choked back tears as she listened to her grandmother speak. Lizzy had said something similar when she came back from the funeral, and on the phone yesterday – that not all of what they had learned from their mother had been true. But Anna had blocked out the possibility. It was too painful to think that she had missed out on time with her father because of a lie. It was easier to hold onto the hatred that she inherited from her mother.

Christos said something to Eirini, who nodded back. He left the room, and Anna sat in a stalemate with her grandmother until he returned a few minutes later with a dusty shoebox. He handed it to Eirini and kissed her on the cheek as she began to cry. She sat quietly with tears streaming down her face for nearly two minutes before nodding and putting her hands on the box.

"These are letters your father sent to your mother. They were all returned unopened. We've never read them, but we've held onto them since he died. Maybe it will help you understand who he was better than you did from your mother." She set the shoebox down in front of Anna. "Now, I think I'm going to go lie down. I will see you soon."

Eirini left the room, and Christos reached into a cupboard and pulled out a plastic food container. He put a little bit of everything they had eaten for dinner inside, along with a few pieces of the baklava Anna had brought. Then he put the lid on, walked over to the door to the courtyard and opened it.

"Goodnight Anna," he said, holding out the container.

Anna picked the shoebox up off the table and walked over to Christos. She didn't enjoy being shouted at by Eirini, but being kicked out by Christos was even worse. She took the container from him and, as she started to step outside, considered giving him a hug, but, with her barely outside, he began shutting the door. She scooted out of the way and through the courtyard as quickly as possible, her cheeks burning red from embarrassment. She went through the gate and through her front door, put the leftovers in the fridge, and sat down at the table with the shoebox.

Inside were several unopened letters, just as Eirini had said. There were also a lot of loose papers, and a few clippings from magazines and newspapers. Anna couldn't read any of that, of course. She was disappointed to see that there were no photos of him inside. She could remember what he looked like when she was younger – despite her feelings about him, she had fought for nearly two decades to hold onto that image – but she had trouble picturing what he would have looked like as he aged. There had been no pictures of him in Eirini and Christos's house, either. It must have been too sad for them.

As she thumbed through the envelopes, Anna saw envelopes addressed to her mother, "RETURN TO SENDER" scrawled across them in big, red letters. She ran her hand over the writing. She couldn't have remembered her father's handwriting until now, but she knew it instantly. Giant lettering, all capitals, just like how he talked. Thick, like he was feeling the weight and heft of every word he wrote. A slight left-hand slant. Words and lines scrunched together. It was him on paper. Anna ran her fingers over the writing, remembering scribbled notes to her and Lizzy that he would leave in their lunch boxes. She felt five years old again.

Maybe Eirini was right. Maybe she couldn't trust what her mother said. If she were being honest, part of her had always known that. She had never been Grace Linton's number-one fan, but it was time to find out for herself where the truth lay.

She dumped all the papers out onto the table and separated the letters – 6 in total, mixed in with some scraps and notes – and sorted them by the date on the postage. She found the first one, dated just a few days after he'd left them. She grabbed a flathead screwdriver from the counter to use as a makeshift letter opener, slicing through the envelope and sending dust into the air. She pulled the yellowed paper from within and unfolded it as she sat down on the bed and began to read.

Dear Grace,

I've been back for less than a week, and I already don't think I can stand it. I understand that you're not happy, but did you have to make up something so terrible about me? If you wanted to get rid of me, couldn't we have just separated? Then I wouldn't be away from my children. I wouldn't be alone on this island. My parents are glad to see me, but they're confused, and I don't know what to tell them.

When you kicked me out, you said that you knew I was cheating on you. I know you were just making a scene to make yourself look like the victim. You're very good at that. But do you understand what that will do to our girls? Even if they didn't hear it when you were shouting, they'll hear it from someone else, assuming you haven't told them already. Please don't lie to my daughters about me. Especially Anna. She's too young. If you tell her I hurt you, that I betrayed the family, she will hate me forever. I know it. Please don't tell them what you said. We both know it's not true, and I couldn't take it, never seeing my girls again because of a lie.

I understand if you don't want us to be together. I know this isn't the life you wanted for yourself. If I'm honest, our life wasn't exactly my ideal, either.

But our girls changed everything for me. I just want to be with them. Please don't petition for divorce. I'll never be able to get back to them, and you know it. I'll live somewhere else, let you have them full-time, just as long as I can see them. You can be with whoever you want, though you don't need my permission. If my suspicions are correct, you've been doing that anyway. But Grace, darling, I don't care about that. I care about you, but I know our marriage is over. Just, please, I'm begging you, let me be a father to our two perfect daughters. I don't know what I am if I can't be that.

Please.

Giorgos

"So, what do you think it means?" she asked. "Do you think it means my mom was the one cheating on him?"

Nikos sighed. "Do you want my honest answer?"

Anna nodded.

"That's what he told me," Nikos continued. "When we spoke about it, he always said that she was the one who wasn't faithful. Not that he was madly in love with her anymore; it seemed like he only stayed married to her for you and your sister. But from what he told me, he never cheated. Why were you so convinced he had?"

Anna shrugged. "I guess when he left, I felt confused and hurt. I was too young to comprehend anything beyond 'he's not here, so he doesn't want to be here.' So when my mother started offering explanations, I channelled all my emotions into those. It was easier to be angry than it was to see both sides, even when the cracks in her story started to show."

"Well, it seems like she fabricated quite a bit."

"I honestly don't know how someone could ever make up something like that," she said, putting down the letter and picking up a crowbar.

The old tiles were almost gone, good riddance. Over the next two days, they planned to tile and grout the floors while Anna stayed at the resort. She had managed to convince Xenia to let her use an empty room, promising to vacate if they had any more bookings. Guests were scarce, though, with the building in the final stages of renovation. They had put a warning on the dates in the booking system, so it was practically a ghost town despite being the start of the summer season. It certainly wasn't doing anything for Anna's tips at the cafe.

"Anyway, what are you up to tonight?" she asked Nikos. "Still playing video games with Kostas?"

"Actually, no," Nikos replied. "He texted me this morning to cancel. He said he wasn't feeling well, but knowing him he has a date or something."

"Oh, I'm sorry." Anna hesitated before continuing. Things were just starting to get better between them again. But maybe that was the reason why she *should* continue.

"You know, I'm not doing anything tonight, either," she said. "Want to watch a movie?"

Nikos glanced up at her and smiled a cocky little grin, and Anna immediately regretted offering. He was sure to think she was hitting on him.

"You're not going to make me watch something dumb, are you?" he asked.

Anna rolled her eyes. "What, like *The Notebook* or *Sleepless in Seattle?*"

"Are you kidding me?" Nikos asked, standing up from the ground. "The Ryans are absolute legends."

"The Ryans?"

"Ryan Gosling and Meg Ryan, obviously," he said with a wink. "No, I meant are you going to make me watch some shitty macho movie because you think it's what I want to watch, so I have to pretend to enjoy it?"

"I would never," Anna said, feigning offense. "How about you pick what we watch?"

"Okay, but I sure hope you're ready for a good cry," he said, bending down to pry the last tile from the floor. "Because if you don't cry every time Jennifer Garner reads one of Gerard Butler's letters, I'm never hanging out with you again."

Anna chuckled and watched as Nikos pulled the final tile free and set it in the wheelbarrow.

"And *fin*," he said, taking a bow. Anna tucked the crowbar under her arm and offered a golf clap.

"Bravo!"

"Thank you very much," he said, standing up and wiping his brow. "Now, if we're going to have a movie night, we'd better get cleaned up."

Anna stopped clapping. "Do you not need to go home?"

Nikos shook his head. "Nope. I've got a change of clothes in the truck."

"Oh, okay," Anna said, desperately trying not to picture

the clothes-changing happening. While she was busy *not* lusting after him, Nikos took the wheelbarrow outside, came back in with a bag, and disappeared into the bathroom.

Anna considered texting Elena to ask her to act as a buffer, but she decided against it. If she and Nikos were going to be friends, they needed to be able to do things together without it being awkward. She just had to make sure they didn't get too cozy while that friendship was still being established.

She stood up and started tidying the room – at least, she tidied as much as she could with the floor fully ripped up. She wiped down all the surfaces, put away the tools, and took the plastic off the bed and sofa.

She heard the water stop and knew Nikos must be getting in the bath, so she forced herself to think about her summer house to-do list instead of the scene in her bathroom at the moment.

The old tiles were ripped out, and the windows had been replaced. They would lay the new tiles next week, and then they could start painting. The new appliances and furniture were at Nikos's so they wouldn't get splattered with paint or grout. The plumber was coming in a couple of weeks to fit the shower and check out the plumbing situation. Now the only things she needed to sort out were the utilities and the driveway, and then she would need to buy decorations and linens.

While she was waiting for Nikos to finish, Anna grabbed

her laptop off the table and settled down on the sofa to check her bank account balance. At least Eirini and Christos were still letting her use the WiFi. She logged into her bank's website and pulled up her accounts. Based on the estimates she'd received, she had just enough to finish what she needed to do before running out of money, and that was if she managed to keep it cheap on the decorations. If her earnings from the cafe stayed the same – so, *low* – then she would just be able to get by until the house sold.

Having logged out of her account, she was about to shut the computer when she noticed the date: June 8. She realized that it was the day her application for the MarMac contest would have sent. She smiled. Part of her hoped it would do well, and obviously winning would be amazing for her career, but, for the first time since she'd arrived, she didn't much care about what the people back home thought of her. It may have been inconvenient, but her time here was definitely giving her some much-needed perspective. People on the island seemed far less concerned with climbing the corporate ladder and reaching the next level than people back home. They cared far more about enjoying the level they were on, and it was starting to rub off on Anna as well. She was spending less time worrying about how she was perceived or what she would do next in life and was enjoying each moment as it happened. Not that she could completely escape thinking about the future, but it certainly wasn't hanging over her head like it usually did.

The water started again, and Nikos emerged in a cloud of steam from the bathroom wearing only a towel wrapped around his waist. There was no need to look through a holey tee shirt this time to see how fit he was.

"I would say something about conserving water, but frankly it was grey by the time I got out, so I've drained it and am refilling it for you."

"Thanks," Anna said, trying not to stare, but he was now standing directly in front of her. She decided to stand up so at least she was eye level with his face instead of what was there now. As she stood, it brought her closer to him. She could feel the heat coming off him, and she wasn't sure if it was from the water, the physical work or the tension.

"Your turn," he said, smiling, but he didn't move out of her way.

"Listen, Nikos," she said quietly, not sure how to articulate what she was thinking – *I'd really love to jump your bones right now, but I don't want to screw up our friendship or hurt your feelings again* – but she was sure that she needed to say something.

"Yes?" he asked, grabbing a piece of her hair that had fallen loose from her ponytail and tucking it behind her ear.

Anna froze on the spot, her heart pounding. She was close enough to see individual water droplets trickling from his hair and down his torso, getting lost under the towel wrapped loosely around her waist. She couldn't let herself go further than that. That towel felt like the point of no return.

She moved away from his touch slightly, and he seemed to take the hint. He took a small step back.

"Sorry," he said, looking at the floor. He looked so disappointed that Anna had to fight the urge to reach out and touch him. Talk about mixed signals.

"No, I'm sorry," she said. "It's not that I don't want—" He looked up at her hopefully. This was coming out all wrong. "It's just that you're a friend. And you and Elena are all I have here. And I don't want to ruin that."

Nikos nodded. "It's okay," he said. "I get it. You don't know how long you'll be here. I don't want to make things more complicated for you than they need to be."

Anna smiled. "Seriously, if you knew how complicated my last relationship was, you'd understand even more." He cocked his head to the side. "I sort of ended up sleeping with my boss. For more than a year. And when I left to come here, I had just caught him with someone else."

"Wow," he said, exhaling sharply. "Yep, that does sound complicated."

"It's just, I promised myself that I wouldn't use anyone the way that he and I used each other. And with my time here limited, it would feel like I was using you."

Nikos laughed. "It's fine, really. You don't have to explain yourself."

"You sure you're not mad?"

Nikos chuckled in response. "What kind of guy would

I be if I was mad that you wouldn't sleep with me? A shitty one, I imagine."

Despite being startled at the fact that he had said aloud that he wanted to sleep with her, Anna laughed, too. "Thank you," she said. "It really does mean a lot to have you here. Especially with everything I'm learning about my dad." She walked over to the table where the envelopes were still laid out in order, the pile of notes next to it. Nikos walked over as well.

"Have you looked through these?" he asked, thumbing through the notes.

"No, between work and the tiles, all I've been able to do is read the first letter a few times. Plus, most of them are in Greek." She walked over to the wardrobe to grab some pajamas, careful to choose the more modest ones. "You're welcome to look through them while I clean up. You can let me know if there's anything interesting."

"Will do," Nikos said, already doing just that.

Anna closed herself in the bathroom and leaned back against the door. Nikos was overwhelming in so many ways. *Of course* she felt something for him; it would be impossible not to. He was kind and funny and smart, he clearly liked Anna, and he was definitely easy on the eyes. But as much attraction as she felt for him, there was affection there, too. Friendly affection. And friendship was a lot less messy for her right now. She could always change her mind later, but they'd never be able to go back if she hooked up with him now. And depending on how long the house took to sell, she could be around for a while. The last relationship she had been in was thoughtless and convenient. There was no affection. Not even respect. She refused to let herself be treated the same way again, and she certainly didn't want to treat Nikos the way Marcus had treated her.

Anna took her clothes off and sank into the warm bath Nikos had started for her, turning off the tap as she got in. She looked over to the window and out at all the lights twinkling their way down to the sea. She let the heat seep into her muscles, loosening them and easing the soreness that had been building all day. Tearing up tiles was hard work, and her arms were grateful for the bath, but the walk to and from work had been having the most noticeable effect, and her legs were always in need of a good soak. She made a mental note to add magnesium bath salts to her list.

After a few minutes in the tub, Anna got out, dried herself off and slipped into her pajamas. The sweatpants had unicorns all over them, and she had gotten the tee shirt for free from some terrible bar in Manhattan when one of their servers spilled beer all down her front. That was when she had first moved there and was trying to actually make friends, before she got together with Marcus and had spent most of her nights either working at the gallery or at his place.

Yep, she had definitely chosen the least sexy outfit she owned. The thought of Marcus had shut things down entirely.

She opened the door and saw that Nikos had finished

getting the place ready. The oven fan was whirring. Two bottles of beer were out on the table, which was set for dinner, her laptop open across the table with the screen dark.

"I was going to get the film loaded," Nikos said, "but I don't know your password. I tried 'password,' but it turns out you're smarter than a lot of people."

Anna smirked as she walked over and typed it in. "And don't you forget it," she said.

She caught a whiff of whatever was in the oven just as a timer went off on Nikos's phone. "What's for dinner? It smells great."

"*Spanakopita*," he replied, pulling it out and placing it on a potholder in the middle of the table. "Spinach pie with feta cheese in filo pastry."

"I know what *spanakopita* is," she said. "It's one of the few Greek foods we serve at the cafe."

"Well then, you know what you're in for." Nikos sat down at the table as Anna pulled up the streaming service. As she logged in, *Mamma Mia!* came up as the recommended option.

"What do you say?"

"Perfect," he said. "We can sing along, and then I can tell you everything that's wrong with it."

Anna laughed. "Sounds perfect."

One hour and forty-nine minutes – plus a couple of minutes from when Nikos insisted that Anna pause the film while he used the bathroom – and four beers each and their *spanakopita* later, Nikos and Anna lay on the bed, flakes of filo from assorted pastries all over every surface in sight.

"I can't believe you cried," Anna said. "I thought you had seen this movie before?"

"I have!" Nikos said. "That doesn't mean I wasn't moved."

"But none of it was sad."

Nikos turned on his side to face Anna. "That doesn't mean it wasn't incredibly emotional. There are other emotions besides sad, you know."

"Whatever," Anna said with a laugh. She could sense that Nikos was still looking at her, but she didn't return the gaze. They had maintained the perfect distance all evening, and she didn't want to ruin it. It felt so tentative, like one wrong move might crumble them. Or at least crumble her resolve.

"Your dad's notes were interesting," Nikos said to change the subject.

"Oh yeah?" This caught her attention. She sat up and looked down at Nikos. "In what way?"

He sat up too, bringing his legs around to cross in front of him. "Well, they were mostly about the summer house," he said. "There's even a plan for what he wanted to do with it to fix it up. Based on the notes, I'd say they're from before he met your mom."

"Can you show me?"

Nikos stood up and walked over to the counter where

he had put everything, grabbed a piece of gridded paper and crossed back to the bed. He handed it to Anna and sat down next to her. Unfolding it, Anna found a sketch of the summer house.

It was laid out the same – that was no surprise, since Anna hadn't changed anything about the layout, and there wasn't really another way to arrange it. But there were also notes all over the paper with arrows pointing to the kitchen, the windows, the tub... and there were actually some bigger differences evident. For one, he had sketched a patio on the front of the summer house with what looked like a trellis, a porch swing and a fire pit. Anna certainly didn't have those things. There was a driveway as well, coming right up along the side, just like Anna had planned to do.

She pointed at some of the notes with arrows. "What do these say?"

"They're mostly just notes about the types of finishes he'd imagined," Nikos said. "Actually, it seems you guys chose the same tiles for the floor."

Anna thought about the stack of tiles in the kitchen – an extra-large square style in an almost terracotta color. She had chosen it because it reminded her of their conservatory back home, which her father had built with his own hands. He must have built the things at their house in Connecticut that he had dreamed for the summer house.

"Why do you think he never did any of this after he came back?" Anna asked. "He was back for like nineteen years before he died."

Nikos sighed. "Well, I never knew your dad before, obviously, but he was never much of the self-improvement type. He always wanted the best for others and helped them achieve their own dreams, but he never seemed to care much when it came to himself."

"But that doesn't make any sense," Anna said, holding up the paper. "He clearly had dreams and plans at one point."

Nikos looked at Anna with a furrowed brow, like there was something he didn't want to say.

"What?" she asked. "Out with it!"

"Well, it seems like whatever happened with your mom, losing his daughters and all... it must have had a pretty major effect on him."

Anna felt herself welling up with emotion at the realization, and clearly Nikos could see it, too.

"No, no, I don't mean that you guys did anything wrong. I just mean that any kind of life event..."

The tears were coming anyway, and there was nothing Anna or Nikos could do to stop them. As they started to flow down Anna's face, Nikos stopped stammering and wrapped her in a hug instead.

"I'm sorry," he said, "I didn't want to say anything."

"I know," she replied, the sound muffled in his shirt. She pulled back. "But you're right. Of course, you are. You think I haven't wondered over the last few months if that's why his health deteriorated? But what could I have done? I was six when he left, and I only had my mother to tell me what had happened."

Nikos put his forehead against hers. "Oh, Anna, nobody blames you for anything that happened to your father. Of course people wish things had panned out differently. That you'd been allowed to visit him. That you hadn't been lied to. But no one thinks it's *your* fault."

Anna began to sob, collapsing into Nikos's embrace. He hugged her shoulders and ran a hand over her hair, shushing her softly. They stayed that way for a while as Anna thought about the letters her father had written. If her mother had lied to her about her father's infidelity, that means she had wasted the rest of her father's life being unjustly angry with him. He had been sitting here halfway around the world in a dingy cottage – something he used to care so much about but toward the end could barely manage to keep clean – knowing that his daughter hated him and knowing that he had done nothing to earn that hate. Despite knowing she was too young to have done any differently, Anna was furious with herself. She had missed out on so much, and there was no way to get it back.

No wonder everyone was hesitant to welcome her. At least Lizzy had come to the funeral. Anna had waited months before swanning over and collecting the house he had left her so she could earn enough money to support herself while she "followed her dreams." What an incredibly privileged and entitled thing for her to expect to be able to do, especially since, from what she understood, most people on the island had never left Greece.

"For the first time, I understand why everyone has been so hostile toward me," she said between sobs. "I would be hostile too if one of my friends had been through all of that only to have his house sold out from under his parents' feet after he died."

Nikos pulled her closer and gently kissed the top of her head. "You have Elena and me, and we don't think that. We know you just want to do the right thing for yourself and your sister. We wouldn't be helping you if we didn't believe that."

"Thank you," Anna said, pushing back so she could look at Nikos. "I know I told you before I was in this alone, but I don't think that anymore. I didn't even think that then. I couldn't do this without you."

Nikos smiled slightly. "I'm not going anywhere."

Anna fell back into his arms as they lay back on the bed. All that effort keeping herself at a distance throughout the evening, and here she was now wrapped up in bed with him. But romance was the furthest thing from her mind. With her mind spinning and her emotions reeling, all she cared about was that for the first time she was lying next to a man that made her feel understood.

11

As Anna locked the door of the summer house, she mentally double-checked that she had everything she would need for the day. It had been so long since she had done any real shooting. She had brought three lenses, two extra batteries, an extra memory card, and a small tripod. She also had a spare dress and a towel with her. The camera equipment was for her shoot with Elena, but Nikos had instructed her to bring a change of clothes as well. Given that he had also told her to wear a swimsuit, she assumed they were getting in the water somewhere, and it was about time. She had been living on an island for weeks and had yet to go in the sea. She had tried to force herself to choose the more conservative one-piece she still had from the summer she spent lifeguarding, but she couldn't resist grabbing her white crocheted bikini instead, throwing it on under a flowy white blouse and denim cut-offs.

She heard the sound of a motorbike pulling up outside, and when she turned around, saw Nikos walking through the gate with a helmet on.

"Um, am I supposed to ride on that thing with you?" she asked.

Nikos grinned. "Come on, it's the perfect day for it!"

Anna laughed and shook her head. "No wonder you drive the truck everywhere you can."

"Come on," Nikos said with a wave. "Elena is meeting us in town."

Anna walked through the gate to see a mint green Vespa parked in the drive. Nikos offered her a helmet, so she took it, put it on, made sure her backpack was secure, and hopped on the back.

This obviously wasn't the first time she had been this close to Nikos, but it was the first time she had been this close without tears streaming down her face, and it was a much different experience. As she wrapped her arms around his waist, she felt how firm his abs were, and the memory of him wearing nothing but a towel flashed through her mind. She tried her best to push it aside, but she also scooted a bit closer to him, pressing herself against his back and inhaling the scent of him. His shirt smelled like fabric softener, but beneath that was the musk of a sweaty – though not smelly – man. She startled when he pushed off and drove the Vespa forward, and her clinging on instantly became less about feeling him up and more about actually staying on the motorbike.

The wind whipped through Anna's hair as they climbed the hills, heading away from the resort. The helmet kept her hair from blowing in her face too much, but still she spent an inordinate amount of time pulling strands from her mouth. Houses and vineyards lined the roads as they twisted and turned. Occasionally Anna would think she caught a glimpse of blue sea through the hills and buildings, but then it would disappear as quickly as it had appeared. Finally they came to what looked like a major road at the top of the hill and turned right. And just like that, the entire caldera was laid out in front of her.

She gasped, craning her neck to see around Nikos and take in every inch of the view. They were in almost the exact middle of the crescent, with the northern tip reaching into the sea in front of them. A channel to the left separated a much smaller island from Santorini proper. Another island, so small it was barely visible, sat further off to the left. Anna craned her neck around and could see that beyond that the other end of the crescent curved around to complete the circle. Boats of all sizes, from big cruise liners to tiny catamarans, were sailing through the channel and around yet another island in the center of the caldera.

Anna could hear that Nikos was trying to say something, but she couldn't hear him over the wind and the engine, so she just admired the view, saying "wow" every now and then in case he was looking for acknowledgment. They were only able to see the caldera for a minute before the road went downhill again, weaving through small clusters of buildings and over the hilly terrain. After a few minutes they came into what Anna recognized as the town of Thera, where she and Nikos had come for supplies, though they had come at it from a different way.

After they passed through the town, they came to a part of the journey where they could only see the sea on the other side. And while there weren't any other islands or any boats to be seen, it was still beautiful. Here the land ran more steeply down to the sea than it did down near the summer house or the resort. There were no buildings along the road, just hills sloping sharply up to the left and down to the right, the Vespa winding around them at what felt like a million miles an hour. It was absolutely exhilarating. This wasn't the postcard version of Santorini, but it was a very real and important part of it, and Anna loved it.

After what must have been about forty-five minutes, Nikos pulled over into a parking lot. "This is where we get off," he said. "We're walking from here." Anna handed over her helmet and followed Nikos through the streets.

As they crossed over an intersection, all of a sudden the town of Oia was laid out in front of them. Beautiful white and yellow buildings with arches and blue domes and infinity pools were clustered together on the hillside so closely that no earth was left to be seen. This was the Santorini Anna had always pictured.

And it was fucking crowded.

Within thirty seconds, Anna was asked to move twice for pictures. It was only nine in the morning! Where had all of these people come from?

"A bit busy, isn't it?" Anna asked, and Nikos laughed.

"I told you," he said. "Bloody influencer wannabes. They come in for the season and take over the town and then disappear, leaving us to deal with the aftermath."

Anna looked up at Nikos, who was making faces at the crowd milling around them.

"Okay, Mr Grinch," she said. "I was more thinking that it's going to be tough to get photos of *your cousin*, who I believe actually wants to be one of these 'bloody influencers.'"

Nikos gave a sarcastic smile before raising his eyebrows and then his hand. He started waving. Anna turned around and saw Elena pushing through the crowds pulling a suitcase behind her.

"Hi, guys," Elena said, kissing them both on the cheek. She looked at Anna. "I didn't know where we would find the best light, so I brought a few different outfits to make sure each photo is cohesive."

Anna eyed the suitcase. "How many is a few?"

"Well, let's see," Elena said, pursing her lips. "I have six dresses— no, make that seven, a few swimsuits, a pair of flowy trousers..."

"I guess it's a good thing we have all day then, isn't it?"

Nikos laughed. "You two have fun. I'm going to work for a bit, but I'll come back when you two are done. Just text me."

"You don't want any photos taken?" Anna asked, pulling her camera out of her bag and winking at him.

"Hah-hah, very funny," he replied as he walked away. The girls waved at him as he left.

"Alright then," Anna said, "I guess we'd better get started."

Four hours later, they were sat at a cafe eating gyros, Elena taking delicate, photogenic bites of hers while Anna snapped away. Being Elena's personal paparazzi was a bit exhausting, but she knew Elena would be returning the favor over the next few days with the tiling project. They had actually gotten a lot of good photos despite the crowds, though a lot of them involved jumping up on people's walls or asking the crowd to hold back. Anna suspected Nikos would not have approved, but that was fine. They were Elena's photos, and she looked stunning in every single one.

At one point, when they were finishing up on a particularly pristine wall with a gorgeous view beyond, a group of girls – seven in total, all in crop tops and white sneakers – stopped and asked if Anna would take their pictures, so she reached out her hand to take their phones.

"No, we mean with your camera," one of the girls said with a strong southern accent. "You could email 'em to me, maybe?"

"Oh, I don't know..." Anna looked at Elena, who shrugged.

"We're happy to pay," the girl added, reaching into her bag. "We're all leavin' tomorrow anyway, and we have a bunch of euros left. Is a hundred enough?"

Anna agreed, took the bills from the girl's hand, and directed her on the wall. She got a few good snaps in different poses and showed them to the girl to make sure she liked them. When they were done, she motioned for the next girl. But instead of stepping up to the wall, she held out 100 euros of her own. Anna looked at Elena, who was grinning like a madwoman. She took the money from the second girl, who then posed on the wall, too. Again, Anna made sure the photos she took were unique enough to justify the payment. Then they followed the group to another spot where some of the girls wanted their photos taken. After she'd taken photos each of them – and they'd each paid her their 100 euros – Anna took out her phone and entered each of their email addresses so she could send them the final shots.

One of the girls tried to give her another 50 euros, but she shook her head. "Don't be silly. If you want, you can give me a photo credit, but even that isn't necessary since you guys paid for these." The girl insisted though, so Anna gave her the handle for the Instagram she hadn't logged into in weeks.

"Unedited JPEGs please," one girl said. "I need to be able to apply my presets." The others all nodded their agreement, but Anna didn't much care what format they wanted – she had walked away with 700 euros more than she'd arrived with that morning.

And now, sitting in the cafe with Elena, she flicked through the photos, amazed that she could earn so much money from something she loved doing. Could she make a living taking pictures of influencers? Probably not. But it was nice to feel valued. It was more than she could say about working with Marcus, anyway.

"Okay, let's just eat normally now," Elena said before taking a giant bite of her wrap, but Anna couldn't resist the urge to snap another photo. Elena heard the shutter and squealed. "Oh my god, you have to delete that!" she said, her eyes wide.

Anna laughed. "Whatever you say." She set the camera down on the table and began to eat.

"So what's the deal with Nikos and 'influencers'?" she asked after a few bites, raising two fingers from her gyro to make the air quotes.

"Ugh, don't even get me started," Elena said. "He's impossible. You get dumped by a few American girls on holiday and all of a sudden all influencers are bad. Despite the fact that the tourism industry has almost always been our primary source of income and we make almost all of our money during the summer—"

"I'm sorry, did you say he's been dumped by a few American girls?"

Elena paused for a moment. "Yes, I did. Why? Is that of interest to you?" She wiggled her eyebrows at Anna and made kissy noises.

"That's not what I meant," Anna asked. "I'm just curi—"

"I know it's not what you *meant*, but is it *true*?"

"Well, yes, it's true that it's of interest to me. I am interested to know."

Elena smiled at Anna wordlessly.

"Oh, shut up and just answer me," Anna said, even though Elena hadn't actually said anything. If it were Nikos sitting across from her, he undoubtedly would have commented by now on how red she was.

Elena nodded and put her food down. "Over the years, Nikos has tried to date a few girls who have come here on vacation. He always catches feelings, but none of them are quite into the storybook idea of living on a tiny fishing island in a foreign country forever, so they leave, and he gets sad. He's sort of learned to just stay away, which manifests as him being annoyed with all of them before they can break his heart."

Anna nodded along as Elena talked.

"Any thoughts?"

"Not really," Anna said. "It's just interesting. He seemed so against all tourists. But if he wants to date someone who's not Greek, why did he stay here? Lizzy told me he has a degree from LSE. Surely he could get a job anywhere in the world and actually have a future with one of these women?"

"Because he's a masochist," Elena said. "He's the one that decides to stay here and to hook up with girls that are here for like a week. He always knows that going into it. He's just a glutton for punishment."

As Elena continued to complain about Nikos's behavior,

Anna thought about how he had acted toward her. He complained about the other tourists, but would he do that to their faces? Or would he flirt with them the way he had with Anna?

"I just don't see why he has to— *ti manari einai autos* Anna. Oh. My. God!"

Anna shook herself out of her thoughts and tried to follow Elena's gaze across the street. "What? What are you looking at? You know I don't speak Greek."

"There," Elena said, reaching across the table to grab Anna's face and point it toward a Greek guy eating an ice cream cone across the street.

"That guy? What about him?"

Elena looked like Anna had just insulted her mother. "He's beautiful. Isn't he *beautiful*?"

He was very muscular, that much was certain. Beautiful wasn't the word Anna would have used, but she could see how someone might find him attractive in a Jersey Shore sort of way, with his greased-back hair and wife-beater top two sizes too small. Thankfully, Elena didn't wait for Anna to answer. Actually, she didn't wait at all. For anything. She just stood up and walked right over to him, flipping her hair over her shoulder and touching his arm. Anna watched mesmerized as they talked, eyeing each other up like two juicy steaks. It was as pornographic as an inaudible conversation could be without any actual sexual contact.

Less than two minutes later, Elena took him by the hand

and pulled him over to Anna, grabbing her purse from her chair.

"Anna, this is Vasilis. He's going to take some pictures with us."

Vasilis nodded. "He is?" Anna asked.

"Of course," Elena said, putting a hand on his chest. "We're just going to go next door and get him a better shirt. Do you want to meet us there in a few?"

"Sure," Anna said, smiling. Before she could ask how long she should give them, Elena pulled him away, and they were gone.

Anna picked up her camera, excited at the idea of a few minutes of solo exploring. Oia was a beautiful town, but Elena was more interested in capturing the sweeping vistas and iconic angles than the details. Anna walked up and down the street snapping photo after photo. She captured two men negotiating the price of the day's catch in front of a restaurant, a girl sitting in a window reading, and a cat lapping at a bowl of milk someone had left out for it.

After about ten minutes, she decided to head back to the shop next to the cafe. But just before she got there, she passed a small alley where Elena and Vasilis were pressed against each other making out. At least Vasilis was indeed wearing a different top.

Anna cleared her throat. "Should I come back?"

Elena looked up, unfazed, as if she were always making out with one person when talking to another.

"Don't be silly," she said. "We're more than ready."

Anna shrugged, and as Elena turned back to give Vasilis another kiss, she snapped a photo. Elena didn't even notice. This was going to be interesting.

The photoshoot with Elena and Vasilis definitely was interesting. It was also incredible. They looked like they belonged on a movie poster or magazine cover. As much as Anna didn't love the muscles, the camera did. Their faces always found the light, their clothes always billowed flatteringly in the wind, and their chemistry was undeniable. In fact, they had started to gather a little crowd of onlookers in front of what Anna now knew was referred to as Three Blue Domes.

"Amazing Elena, try throwing your train up again." Elena was wearing a white swimsuit cover-up with slits up both sides, creating a train in the back. She had her left leg poking out of it, and she threw the train out behind her into the wind as she kissed Vasilis.

"Yep, just like that," Anna said, capturing shot after shot. She looked down for a split second to check the shutter speed, and the image was so bright and crisp she thought she may not need to edit it at all.

"I leave you for one day and you've got my cousin making out with random guys for a photo op?"

Anna spun around to see Nikos standing behind her, looking over her shoulder.

"Nikos! I didn't know you were here. How did you know where to find us?"

He gestured toward Elena, who didn't seem to notice that the camera had stopped watching her since she was still posing as she kissed Vasilis. Then again, that didn't seem particularly out of character. "Juliet Capulet over there texted me. Said she'd need to go soon."

"Oh," Anna said with a frown, "I didn't realize she was going anywhere. We've still got so much good light."

"Sorry," Elena said, trotting over. "I have to work at the bar tonight, so I called in a replacement." She took her cover-up off and pulled her work shirt and shorts out of her bag. The first public change had shocked Anna, but after over a dozen of them she was used to it now.

"You've worked evening shifts every night for the last week," Anna said. "You must be raking it in."

"It's been alright," Elena said. "It'll be even better when the resort has its grand re-opening next week. I'm working every night until then, too. Except grout night, of course." Grout night was what they had started to call the evening they planned to grout Anna's floors.

"And Wednesday night," Nikos added.

"Um, no, I'm working Wednesday," Elena said, looking confused.

Nikos threw up his hands. "What about the wedding?"

Elena's eyes went wide. "Oh, Nikos, I completely forgot. I am *so*, so sorry."

He rolled his eyes. "Myrto is going to be furious if there's an empty seat. She asked me to confirm like three times."

"Take Anna, then," Elena said, nodding toward her.

"Uh, sorry, what's this?"

"Yes, great idea," Nikos said. "She'll be a better date than you, anyway."

Elena laughed. "Nobody's a better date than I am, even if I am your cousin. She will do, though."

"Thanks a lot," Anna said. "Now what have I been roped into?"

"It's just a wedding," she replied. "Just find a dress that's not white, and Nikos will pick you up. Sound good?"

"A wedding on a Wednesday? Isn't that a bit non-traditional?"

"This coming weekend is a holiday, so they had to do it midweek to use the church."

Anna nodded. "Sounds good," she said. "I'm in. It'll give me an excuse to show off my dance moves."

Elena hugged Anna, kissed Nikos on the cheek and turned back to Vasilis, who had sauntered over. She took his phone out of his pocket, put her number in it, and returned it to him. "Call me," she said to him, then, to Anna and Nikos, "see you guys later." And then she was gone, suitcase dragging behind her.

Nikos said something to Vasilis in Greek. Vasilis nodded at Nikos, then at Anna, before leaving.

"What did you say to him?" Anna asked.

"Just that I wouldn't be making out with him for photos, so he should probably call it a night."

Anna laughed. "Alrighty, then, should we head back?"

"Well, wait a minute," Nikos said, "I doubt that you've

gotten to experience much of the town while taking pictures of madam supermodel."

"That's true…"

"I didn't have you bring a swimsuit for nothing. Why don't we do a bit of exploring?"

Anna nodded, let her camera rest around her neck, and followed Nikos back into the streets of Oia. As they wandered, they snacked on *koulouri*, a circle-shaped sesame breadstick they had bought from a street vendor, and ducked in and out of a few shops alongside the other tourists: one specializing in artisan olive oils, one that sold locally made ceramics, and a bookstore called Atlantis Books that was tucked underneath another building.

"Did you know that Santorini was actually the origin of the myth of Atlantis?" Nikos said as Anna stared down at the orange and blue storefront.

"Really? But I thought Atlantis was meant to be underwater?"

"Yes, well, the island used to all be one, and people lived all over it," Nikos said. "When the volcano erupted, it then collapsed in on itself, creating the caldera. That's the underwater part."

"That's so cool," Anna said, stepping down into the shop. A cat curled around her feet as she walked inside. Books were stacked floor to ceiling against every surface, held up by rustic wooden shelves, each one different.

She followed the signs for English fiction and picked up a couple of summery-looking reads, taking them to the checkout counter. Once she'd paid for them, she put them in her camera bag along with a candlestick she had bought from the ceramics shop.

They wove slowly side by side through the town, making their way down toward the water. But all of a sudden, the road just stopped, and they were at a drop-off that went straight down into the water. "So, where to now?" Anna asked, but she already knew the answer. Nikos confirmed with the direction he pointed. They were headed down.

Two hundred fourteen steps later, they were at a small bay lined with buildings. Sailboats were moored in the center, and a few people swam amongst them. The water was a deep, rich blue, almost completely still except for gentle rippling on the surface.

Anna heard a shout and turned to the left to see a girl hurtling through the air toward the water. She flailed around, screaming, before plunging into the bay feet first. Anna gasped, but then she heard cheering and realized that there was a small group of people a little ways up one of the cliffs on a massive boulder, a tiny path winding up it toward them. Suddenly, Anna understood what they were there to do.

"Um, I think I left something in the Vespa. I'm gonna go back up," she said.

Nikos laughed. "You did not leave anything in the Vespa, and you're not walking up hundreds of steps to escape one itty bitty jump. My friend at the taverna over there told me we can leave our things with him, and the water is plenty deep. You have nothing to worry about."

"Yeah, see, you're wrong about that," Anna said, but she didn't leave. She didn't go toward the jump, either, but she didn't leave. She stayed planted, terrified, in place. Though Nikos was actually helping. Making her feel calmer. Calm enough to jump off a cliff, though? That remained to be seen.

They pulled off their clothes, and Anna saw Nikos notice her bikini, then try to look away subtly. She didn't hate being appreciated after all the leering she'd done over the last few weeks.

The drop looked so much higher the further up the rock they climbed and, as they got to the top, Anna froze. She had come all this way to Greece to what, sit around and paint cabinets? No, part of her had wanted an adventure. But jumping off the rock with Nikos felt like more than just swimming. It felt like abandon, which was something she had been trying to avoid since she had landed. Since her father had left, actually.

"Come on," Nikos said. "Have an adventure with me." He held out his hand and smiled at her.

Then again, how was she supposed to say no to that? Gathering herself together, she put her hand in his and nodded. "Okay. Let's jump."

"I cannot believe you made me do that," Anna said, taking a sip of her beer.

"Oh, come on, it was cute when you screamed." Nikos laughed and called the waiter over, then looked out over the water. Quickly, Anna brought the camera up to her eye and snapped a picture. The click of the camera made Nikos turn around. "Hey, no paparazzi," he said, sticking out his hand. "Let me see."

"No way," she said. "I never let people see my work before I'm ready."

"Well, I didn't sign a model release form," he said, "so I get veto power."

"Fine," Anna mumbled, handing him the camera. The waiter came over and took their order as Nikos scrolled through the photos from the day.

"These pictures are amazing," he said. He took a sip of his drink and put it back on the table, sitting up straight like he was debating whether or not to say something. "You're really talented, Anna."

"Thanks," she said, shrugging. She figured that he probably felt that he had to say that.

"No, really," he said. "You could totally take photos for a living. I bet a lot of people on the island would hire you, especially the resorts and the businesses that cater to tourists."

"Yeah, well, I don't really want to spend my summer building a photography business just to have to start from scratch when I go home." Anna said this casually, but when she looked up, she could tell that it wasn't the response Nikos had been hoping for, and suddenly everything clicked into place.

"You mean so that I wouldn't *have* to go home," she said. She looked at him expectantly, waiting for him to confirm or deny what she had just said, but he just looked back out at the water and frowned. Anna sighed. She thought about what Elena had said about the girls he had dated and wondered if he had been like this with them.

"Listen, Nikos. I can't just stay in Greece forever. I have a life back home."

"Do you, though?" he asked, turning back to her. "You said that you don't have a job, a place to live, or any real friends there. Your sister lives hundreds of miles away, and you don't get along with your mother. What do you have there that you don't have here?"

"Um, I don't know... citizenship?" Anna said, but he did have a point. She had actually done some research before getting her job at the cafe, and she was automatically a Greek citizen because of her dad. She just had to apply. She had been thinking of this summer as a layover on her way to the next stage of her life, and she couldn't forget about all the work ahead of her to get her to that place. But what if Santorini wasn't the layover but the destination? What if she didn't have to go back to the life that left her feeling empty and worthless? Wouldn't that be worth considering?

"This doesn't have to be just an extended vacation," Nikos said. "You have family here. Friends. A job with someone who doesn't manipulate you. Find a few photography clients, and you could build a life here."

It was Anna's turn to look out at the water to avoid eye contact. Nikos was making a lot of sense, but it wasn't sitting right with Anna. Yes, she could probably find a way to stay in Santorini long-term. But would she be doing it for herself? For her friends? For a job? Or would she be doing it for a guy? She had told Nikos that she wouldn't use him, but equally she didn't want to change her plans for him. Not that she had any particular plans; she had been feeling adrift ever since she'd arrived. But forming plans around people she had known for just a couple of weeks seemed foolish, even if she had nothing else to plan for.

"I don't think so, Nikos." She went to take another sip of her beer, but it was empty. "I'm having a great time today, and I hope we can be friends," she said, reaching across the table to touch his hand, but thinking twice about the signal it might send and setting it on the table instead. "You and Elena are the first real friends I've had in a while, and I want to spend this summer with you. You make me feel like me, and I didn't even really know what that felt like before I came here. But I plan to leave when the house sells. There's too much pain here for me."

Nikos looked up, and she caught his gaze and held it for a moment. He looked sad, but like he understood as well. "Of course," he said. "You have to do what's right for you."

The two turned their gazes back to the water, where the sun was beginning to set. Anna watched it lower over the caldera and sink below the horizon, casting a glorious rainbow of color on the clouds and the buildings and the water. But despite their conversation, she wasn't thinking about how her days of watching sunsets here were numbered. She was just enjoying the moment with her friend, and with herself. Her *actual* self, the one who jumped off cliffs and ate lots of pastries and cared about more than her career and her social image. The self that she hadn't seen in a long, long time.

The cafe was usually quiet on Mondays, so Anna was able to close up a bit earlier than expected. Nikos had offered her a ride home, so she decided to sit down on a pool chair and lay in the sun until he finished his shift.

As she powered up her phone, she saw an email notification pop up. Her email was usually pretty quiet, so she opened it quickly to see what it was.

What she saw nearly made her drop her phone into her open mouth.

TO: Anna Linton <anna94linton@gmail.com>
FROM: Marcus MacMillan <marcus@marmacgalleries.com>
DATE: 24 June 2019, 15:03
SUBJECT: Well played

Hi Anna,

Imagine my surprise when the winner I picked last night for the Emerging Talent Contest ended up being you. My assistant was absolutely shitting herself when I came in this morning, afraid to tell me. I had to think about what to do, but ultimately you earned this. You're the winner. There'll be a more formal email later offering you the placement, but I just wanted to say, WELL PLAYED. I definitely didn't see that coming.

See you soon,
Marcus

Anna could hardly believe the words she was reading. With everything she had going on, she had pretty much forgotten about the contest. Now she had won it!

Her first thought surprised her: that she would have to leave Santorini in order to accept. Of course she would. But she had been planning to do that anyway, right? Maybe it was the sudden end date to her time here that had her feeling panicked. But it didn't matter. If anything, it made things easier.

Her next thought was about Marcus. What would it mean to accept this from him? She had been proud of herself for standing up to him before she left. She knew she had done the right thing by quitting. Sure, the winner was chosen anonymously, as always, but was this just running back to him and the life she'd left behind? Or was it the opposite, where she had left on her own terms and was somehow being rewarded for it, by him and by the universe?

Either way, she knew what she had to do. It was everything she had wanted for so long. All of those days spent in the gallery gazing at the names of the photographers whose work was on display, every time she had submitted her work somewhere only to be told it wasn't what they were looking for... it was all worth it for this moment. She had won. And she'd be a fool to say no.

Without another thought, she scrolled through to the next email, the formal offer Marcus had mentioned, and responded with just two words:

I'm in.

13

Anna balanced carefully at the bow of the small speed-boat and leaned forward, feeling like Rose and Jack on the *Titanic*. Though hopefully this vessel wouldn't end up on the bottom of the caldera. Luckily, the seas weren't exactly littered with icebergs. They certainly would have all melted by now.

The breeze hitting Anna's face provided some much-needed respite from the heat of the sun, and the occasional splash of water on her face felt like heaven. Her tee shirt stuck to the sweat on her back and stomach, and her thighs were red from rubbing together in the heat. Summer in Greece was officially next-level hot, and they hadn't even experienced the heatwave that was expected, so when Nikos offered a day on the water, Anna was glad to accept.

"You cooling down up there?" Nikos shouted from the steering wheel. Anna put both thumbs up in response. You couldn't have paid her to go back to the stern, where she could practically feel the rays of sun burning the back of her neck. The journey to the volcanic island in the center of the caldera only took a few short minutes, but she would be spending all of it here, at the front of Nikos's friend's boat, making as big a surface area as possible for the breeze to hit.

A few minutes passed like this, Anna with her arms stretched out, before the boat slowed.

"We here?" Anna asked, opening her eyes to see that they were pulling into a small harbor. She climbed back to where Niko was stood.

"Yep, we're here," Nikos replied, easing the boat up next to a slightly larger one and tying onto it. He checked his knots before motioning for Anna to step across to the next boat. She took his hand and stepped over, slowly making her way across the makeshift flotilla to the dock.

As they reached solid ground, Nikos reached into the backpack he was carrying and pulled out some sunscreen and a bottle of water. "We're going to be on this rock for a bit," he said, motioning uphill, "so let's lather up, okay?"

Anna nodded and turned around so Nikos could rub sunscreen on her neck before returning the favor for him. She peered down into the backpack as she did.

"What else you got in there?"

Nikos shrugged. "Oh, you know, the basics. Lots of water. Change of shorts. Snacks. Spare phone battery pack. Your camera."

Anna nodded. "You're very prepared. You should have been a Boy Scout or something."

"Yeah, well, we don't have them here," he said, "but Elena and I did try camping out here when I was about fourteen."

Anna laughed at the thought as Nikos picked up the backpack and started walking up the hill. She walked alongside him along the narrow path, squeezing against him as they passed a couple coming the other way. "How did that go?"

"Not well," Nikos said, "or rather not at all. They clear the island every night. We tried to hide in a cove, and we thought we'd gotten away with it, but as we pitched our tent someone spotted us from the water and called the authorities."

Anna laughed, feeling like she could picture it perfectly: Elena getting angry that someone had caught them, Nikos pretending like it was a good thing, and both of them deciding they hadn't wanted to do it that much to begin with. She and Lizzy had been the same way growing up. She felt a pang of jealousy that Nikos and Elena still had their adventure buddies when hers had moved so far away, before she decided she was glad Nikos was taking her on those adventures. At least for now. She made a quiet promise to herself to go on more adventures by herself when she got home.

As they climbed higher up on the hill, Anna caught glimpses of the view from different angles. But after about twenty minutes, she found herself surrounded by the gorgeous turquoise waters of the caldera in a three-sixty view of Santorini. The colors blended perfectly from sea to sky, and Anna felt like she was on top of the world. Or in it, or over it. All she could see was blue water and blue sky and the earth beneath her feet and the three islands that formed the ring around them. She tried to imagine Santorini as one big island, but she couldn't quite build the picture in her mind. This view was perfection, and she couldn't imagine it existing any other way.

"This is so stunning," she said, her voice barely above a whisper.

"Isn't it?" Nikos said from right next to her, and when she looked at him, she saw that he had his eyes closed and a huge grin plastered across his face. Not directed at her, not because he was pleased at his own cleverness... no, this was pure, unabashed love for his home. She understood perfectly from that look why he had wanted to get back here so badly after university.

"The view's out there," he said without opening his eyes. Anna blushed. *Busted.*

"I just like the way you look at this place," Anna said. "You grew up here, but you're seeing it as if it's for the first time."

"Yeah, well, you did the same thing, didn't you? With those pictures of New York City?"

Anna nodded. "Yeah, but that's not really the same thing, is it?"

"I think it is. It's being able to look past what you know and see what is."

"Very profound."

Nikos chuckled. "I try."

They stood there for a few minutes just basking in the view before Anna pulled out her camera, taking pictures from every angle she could manage. As they headed back down to the boat, she took a few more of the rocky terrain, sneaking a few of Nikos into the mix. She even sat behind the windscreen in the boat as they pulled away so she could take photos from there.

Next they came to the tiny island of *Nisis Palaia Kameni*, just behind the central island. As they approached the island, Anna noticed the color of the water changing. They moored the boat where the water was still turquoise, but instead of going onto the land, Nikos took off his top and jumped in, swimming into a cove where the water turned orange. Anna grimaced, not sure what they were getting into, but she saw others swimming as well, so she followed along, folding her tee shirt and shorts on the seat before jumping in after him.

As she plunged into the water, the cold nearly knocked the breath right out of her, but it felt amazing after a day spent mostly in the heat. She surfaced, looking around before seeing Nikos waving at her from several meters ahead.

As she followed him into the orange-colored cove, a couple of things happened. First, the water got a lot more crowded. The further in they went, the more people there were. Second, there were orange chunks floating past her. This wasn't hugely appealing, but it was probably from all the people kicking up the mud.

The third thing was perhaps the most disconcerting, however: as they swam further into the cove, the water got warmer and warmer. At first, Anna thought it was because it was getting shallower, but after a while it passed the point to which the sun could have heated it.

"Why is the water so warm?" she asked as she caught up with Nikos.

"It's a hot spring," he said. "The water comes from the end of the cove."

Anna rolled her eyes. "It's like a million degrees out and you brought me to a *hot spring*?"

Nikos shrugged exaggeratedly as he treaded water next to her. "I mean, we had the boat for the day, and it's a thing that a lot of tourists like to do."

Anna sighed. As horrible as the idea of a natural jacuzzi sounded at the moment, Nikos was trying to make sure she got the full experience. "Alright, let's go then," she said. "I'll race you to the end!"

Anna and Nikos swam as fast as they could toward the spring. Anna expected to have to stop when it got too hot, but the reality was that they couldn't get anywhere near the end of the cove because of all the people.

"Sorry," Nikos said as they came to a halt. "I tried to time it so we wouldn't be here at the same time as the boat cruise, but there are just too many at this time of year. There's always someone here."

"That's okay," Anna replied, touching his arm. "It's the thought that counts. Plus, I'm absolutely burning up now."

"What do you say we get back on the boat?" Nikos said. "I could do with a drink of water."

"Sounds good."

They took a much more leisurely swim back to the boat and, as they arrived, Anna took a moment to just float on her back under the big blue sky.

"The water feels amazing out here," she said, bumping up against Nikos with her leg. He tilted back as well, holding a rope attached to the boat and hooking his foot on Anna's, connecting them as the waves bounced them up and down. "Who's the Greek god of the sea?"

"Poseidon, I think," Nikos answered, "but that's not still a thing."

Anna laughed. "I know, but I can never remember Greek mythology."

"Well, he wasn't just the god of the sea. He was one of the supreme gods of Olympus. I think he was the god of earthquakes and horses, too."

"And yet he's only known for the sea. Seems like he should have spent more time causing earthquakes or as a horse or something."

Nikos paused for a moment. "I guess you could say he was a bit of a one-trick pony."

Anna burst out laughing, causing her to stop floating,

but she couldn't help it. Nikos laughed too, clearly pleased with himself.

"That is such a dad joke," she said, splashing him with water.

"Yeah, well, clearly it worked." He used the seawater to slick back his hair and smiled at Anna, his white teeth and tanned skin in such contrast in the midday sun. "You ready for lunch?"

"Sure," Anna replied, following Nikos to the back of the boat and up the ladder. Nikos started the boat and untied it from the neighbouring vessel, slowly navigating through the throngs of swimmers and their boats back out onto the open water. But instead of heading back to Oia, he guided the boat further away, toward the smallest ring island of *Aspronisi*.

"Why are we going out here?" Anna asked. "I didn't think you could go to *Aspronisi*."

"Most people can't," he said, pulling into a small natural harbor. "It's been privately owned by the same family for six or seven generations. But I just happen to be friends with that family."

Anna looked at Nikos, her mouth wide. "Seriously?"

Nikos nodded. "Yep. Where do you think I got the speedboat?" He lowered the boat's anchor since there was nothing to moor it to, then jumped out of the boat, ready to swim to shore, the water almost up to his chin when he stood.

"Hand me the backpack and the cooler under the seat,"

he said to Anna, who grabbed the items and passed them to him. He held them over his head. "Now can you bring the towels, do you think?"

Anna nodded, setting the towels on the back of the boat and climbing into the water. Nikos may not have had Boy Scouts, but she had been a Girl Scout, and treading water for three minutes with one arm above her head had been a requirement for her Stage Five Swimmer's Badge. She made her way to the side of the boat, where she could touch the bottom, then walked the rest of the way in.

As they arrived at the pebbly beach, which was otherwise empty of any sign of civilization, Anna spread out the towels. Nikos opened the cooler, taking out a big container of salad, a smaller one of olives, a bag with two sandwiches inside, two forks and two bottles of water.

As they ate lunch, Nikos told Anna about how he knew his rich friend from school, and Anna told Nikos about the Girl Scout camp she had gone to every year from age five to eighteen. When she mentioned the types of badges she had earned, Nikos joked about how sexist it sounded. Anna just laughed before telling him about the science, public policy and environmentalist badges she had gotten, too, and how the most important one by far was her photographer badge.

"Is that how you got into photography?"

Anna nodded. "I was eleven, and it was the best thing I had ever done. All I had was the troop leader's old film camera, but I remember the first picture I ever took. It was of my sister Lizzy doing her homework. She was always so interested in science and agriculture, and she had a workbook open in front of her with a pencil in one hand and a turnip in the other. I thought it was hilarious when I took it, but later when I developed it, I realized the look on her face. She looked determined and passionate, which I had never noticed in her before. And that's when I learned that photography can help you see truths that you would otherwise never notice, even if the subject was right in front of you. Taking a photo of something imbues it with importance, and you're more likely to think about and examine something critically if you think it's important."

"I get that," Nikos said. "I used to wonder when I was living in London how people could see photos of poverty that would break their hearts but walk past it every day in the city without a second glance. I guess what you're saying was probably at play."

"Exactly. Some people don't care about a story until an artist or journalist or social media influencer tells them to. Photography is one way to get people to pay attention to something they might otherwise overlook."

Nikos smiled. "That's really cool. I feel like I understand now why you're so passionate about it."

Anna smiled and felt her face flush. "Thanks," she said. "I really love it. Even taking pictures of Elena on people's garden walls is exciting to me. It may not be drawing attention to poverty, but it helps her feel empowered and important. And I think everyone deserves to feel that way, especially someone as badass as Elena."

Nikos rolled his eyes. "I promise you, she feels plenty important," he said, "but I think it's really great that you feel that way."

Anna popped an olive into her mouth. "Thanks," she said, using her need to chew as a way to avoid having to say more. Instead, she stared out at the water and thought about the MarMac contest for the first time that day. For a moment, she felt like she should just tell Nikos about it. Surely he'd understand now that he knew why photography was so important to her. But, deep down, Anna knew that he would only feel one way with her if she revealed that their time together had an expiration date: disappointed.

After lunch, Anna and Nikos took one more dip in the water before heading back to the main island. They dropped the key to the boat with someone in the harbor office then climbed up to Oia where the truck was parked. They had to go back to the summer house to change so they could go to dinner with Eirini and Christos. Nikos was trying to help Anna stitch her relationship with them back together, and this dinner was a step in the right direction.

As they drove back, Anna knew that she was being evasive. Ever since the email had come through from Marcus, she had known that she would have to tell Nikos and Elena. They might even be happy for her. But part of her felt like they wouldn't be, and that part held her back from saying anything. So she turned up the music in the truck, knowing that if she didn't Nikos would catch onto her lack of desire for conversation and know something was wrong. She wasn't used to having someone other than Lizzy who could read her moods like that. Until she figured out how and when she wanted to tell him, she would have to be careful not to let on that there was anything to hide.

They arrived back at the house, and Anna ran inside to quickly change. Nikos had the decency to change in the main house; after a day of bonding, Anna wasn't sure she could handle a naked Nikos in the summer house. She slipped on as short and skimpy a dress as she deemed appropriate for dinner with her grandparents, not to impress Nikos but to beat the heat – or so she told herself.

Once she was dressed, she locked up the summer house and went to the drive. Eirini and Christos were sat in the cab of the truck, with Nikos in the back. Anna climbed in with him slowly, trying not to moon Nikos as she did. After much awkward dress holding and testing of foot placement, she was in, and Christos began to back down the drive.

"Isn't this delicious?" Eirini said, pointing to the *feta me meli* on her plate. Anna had ordered the same, a pastry parcel filled with feta and drizzled with honey. They served it as a starter at the cafe, but this version was massive, with roasted peppers and mushrooms and spinach inside as well. All of the food at the restaurant was pretty fancy, in fact. They were on the southern rim of the main island, overlooking the caldera as the sun began to set.

"So good," Anna said. "I never would have thought to put honey on veg like this, but it's really yummy."

Eirini smiled and took another bite. The last few days since their less-than-successful family dinner had been much better. Perhaps she felt bad for the way she spoke to Anna. Or maybe she just trusted that Anna had read the letters and come around. While Anna had only been able to read one letter so far, it had certainly helped her view of her father.

With the gallery placement not starting for almost six weeks, Anna had decided she would stay in Greece for as long as possible. It would take a while longer to get the summer house fixed up and sold, and she was enjoying her time here. Plus, until the placement began, she didn't really have anything to go back for. If she was going to be sticking around, it would be nice to be friendly with Eirini and Christos, and she suspected she would continue to need their help.

"About the other night," Anna said to Eirini, but her grandmother wagged a finger at her.

"No, don't say another word. I was unreasonable. I am so sorry for raising my voice."

"I appreciate that," Anna said, smiling. "But I also know that I blindsided you with my plans to sell the house. I'm sorry. I should have made my plans clear from the beginning."

Eirini put her fork down and glanced at Christos, who was deep in a conversation with Nikos in Greek, before responding. "Anna, you don't owe us anything. Your father wanted you to have that house, and we should have listened to his wishes from the beginning. We're just glad that we can get to know you while you're here, and, hopefully, that you can get to know your father a bit better as well. He really was a good man."

"Yeah, well, I'm beginning to get that picture," Anna said. "It's certainly not what's been painted for me by my mother. But thank you for those letters. They are helping a bit."

Eirini nodded and put a hand on Anna's forearm for just a moment. It was the first time that Eirini had touched her, and it surprised Anna for a moment. She looked up at Eirini, who looked like she was beginning to tear up. Seeing Eirini not as her father's mother or as her hostess, but, for the first time, truly as her grandmother, Anna leaned over and hugged her. In response, Eirini wrapped her arms around her granddaughter, rubbing Anna's back as they rocked gently back and forth.

When Anna sat up and smiled at Eirini, she noticed that Nikos and Christos had stopped talking and were looking at them. Nikos was trying to be subtle, looking at his plate and glancing up as he took a bite, but Christos was just beaming across the table at them.

They all went back to eating their dinner, and a few minutes later the rest of the patrons began to crowd around the balcony where they were seated. A famous Santorini sunset was about to begin.

Anna turned around to watch the sun descend slowly toward the horizon and wished for a moment that she had her camera. But she knew she didn't need to take a photo of this moment to make it important. For the first time in the two and a half weeks since she had arrived, Anna felt like she had inherited more than just a house. She had inherited a family.

Hi Grace,

With what would have been our tenth anniversary coming up, I've been thinking a lot about our wedding lately. How it foreshadowed what was to come. How I should have seen it coming.

When you told me you would marry me, I should have been the happiest man in the world. But I wasn't. I was terrified. You had left me once, and though you said it was because you were afraid of your feelings, I don't think I ever fully believed that. Not really. And I knew that if you wanted to you could leave me again. Even then I understood that I was a puppet on a string, and you were the one pulling it.

Not that I didn't want to marry you. When you told me you were pregnant with Lizzy, I could have died of happiness then and there. I was so excited to be a father. It's the greatest joy of my life, even now, after nearly two years away, knowing I probably won't see them until they're old enough to get here on their own. But I was excited to have a baby with you, and I wanted us to be a team. I wanted to know that you would be there for me the way I knew I would be there for you. And that's what I thought our marriage would be.

I should have known, though. Even the way you said, yes, with tears in your eyes not quite convincing as tears of joy. The way you insisted we keep it small, getting married with just your parents at the local church despite your friends having lavish weddings every other weekend. The way you cried every night and told me it was the hormones. I wanted to believe you, but I think I knew deep down that that wasn't it.

I went to a wedding here this weekend. It was a small one, even by Santorini's standards, but it was so happy and full of joy. Everyone dancing together, laughing, celebrating what we all knew was true love. You and I never had that. And if I had been paying attention, if I hadn't been fooling myself, maybe I could have seen that in time to stop what was happening. I could have kept us from growing to resent each other so fully that the only way out was to blow things up. I'm sorry for my ignorance. I'm sorry I was never honest with myself or with you.

Please, Grace. I'm begging you. Please let me see my children. The summer house you stayed in all those years ago is still here. Just say the word and I'll have it ready. I can stay with my parents, and you and the girls can come stay in the cottage. Just please let me see them. It's all I want.

Giorgos

14

"Aaaaand... done!" Nikos said, slotting the last tile into place and standing up. They had strategically tiled themselves right out of the summer house so they wouldn't have to walk on any of the fresh flooring as they left, so they were standing just outside the door. Anna was just coming back from putting her bags in the truck.

"You're my hero," she said, high-fiving him. "There's no way I could have finished this by myself."

Nikos flexed his arms, and Anna laughed. She looked at her phone to check the time.

"Well, we're right on schedule. Maybe we should go get me checked into my room?"

"Sure," Nikos said. "Let's go." They walked to the truck and got in.

"So anything I need to expect for tonight?" Anna had done a bit of Googling about Greek weddings – and had resisted the urge to watch *My Big Fat Greek Wedding* as research – but it seemed that it could be vastly different depending on the couple, the region, the religious denom-

179

ination... basically, her research had done her absolutely no good.

"Hmmm, let's see. Long ceremony, people dancing in circles... what color is your dress?"

Anna paused to recall what she had packed. "Blue."

"That's a stroke of luck," Nikos said. "It's not necessary to wear blue, but a lot of guests will. It's a superstitious thing."

"Lucky I packed it then."

"Also, bring some cash with you. There's a dance at the end of the night where you're meant to throw it at the bride and groom."

"Like they're strippers or something?" Anna asked, shocked.

Nikos laughed. "Honestly? Yeah, a lot like that."

"Weird," Anna muttered, but she was determined to embrace tradition. She thought back to the comment Elena made when Anna cut her foot. "No smashing plates?"

"Not usually. Too dangerous. But I guess it depends on how drunk the *koumbaro* gets. And given that it's Kostas, I imagine that will be *very*."

"Holy shit," Anna said as she opened the door to her hotel room. For some reason, Xenia had offered to upgrade her to one of the new rooms if she checked to make sure everything was okay with it. Anna agreed immediately, especially since this meant she got to have a room service breakfast each morning.

What she didn't anticipate was how incredible the room would be. The ceilings must have been twenty feet high at the tallest point, with crossed arch domes over every room area. A wide hallway with closets on one side led into a massive open room, with a lounge at one end and a massive four-poster bed at the other. Anna peeked into the bathroom and saw a massive freestanding tub, a vanity with lights all around the mirror, and the most incredible rain shower. She actually shuddered with excitement at the idea of an actual shower.

"Nikos, come look at this," she said, waving him over. But when she turned around, she saw him taking his clothes off. "What the hell are you doing?" she asked, not sure whether to look away or go stop him. But before she could decide, in just his shorts he ran out through the patio door and splashed into the pool.

Anna had been so distracted by ceilings and showers that she hadn't even realized there was a private infinity pool on her patio overlooking the sea. She stepped outside and laughed when she saw Nikos splashing around like a kid.

"Come on, get in!" he shouted from the pool.

"No way," she said, shaking her head and staying well out of the splash zone. "I have to get ready for this wedding. One of us should probably look presentable."

Nikos rolled his eyes. "Okay, but at some point over the next three days you have to come swim out here with me."

"The second I don't have anywhere to be, I will," she said, then turned back to the room to start unpacking her clothes.

"Why are you unpacking?" Nikos called from the pool. "You're only here for three nights. Surely you don't need enough clothes to require unpacking."

Anna shrugged. "I always unpack when I go somewhere. I don't like living out of a suitcase." *And I'm a chronic over-packer,* she thought. She turned to look at Nikos, who was dripping wet in the doorway. "Nikos, you're soaking the floor!" she said, running into the bathroom and grabbing a towel. She threw it to him across the room.

He wrapped it around himself and walked toward the bathroom. "Okay, calm down. I'll dry off and get out of your hair." He shut the door behind him.

Anna rolled her eyes and walked over to her bag. She spotted her camera and decided to take a few shots of the room. Her grandfather's crew had done an incredible job. It was the nicest hotel room she had ever been in. She crouched low in front of the TV to get a good shot of the sofa, bed and ceiling. Then she moved Nikos's pile of clothing and took a picture of the lounge. She even arranged some of the toiletries on the bed and took some shots of them.

Next, she decided to take a couple of the patio outside before Nikos did any more damage, so she walked toward the door. As she did, Anna stepped in the water Nikos had tracked in and started to slip. For a moment, she was able to balance herself, but her camera flew up and over her head, and as she reached out her hands to grab it, she was knocked off balance again and tumbled backward toward the cement floor.

Just at the last moment, Nikos appeared beneath her, breaking her fall. She landed on top of his legs, her hand flying up and hitting him in the eye as she gripped her camera.

"Are you okay?" he asked as she rolled off him onto the floor, quickly checking her camera and lens for any damage. She noticed that her fingers were a little tender.

"Yeah, I'm fine, I just— holy shit!" she said, looking up at Nikos. His eye was completely red where she had slammed into it. Her stomach dropped. All this time trying not to hurt Nikos emotionally and she had managed to injure him physically. She put her camera on the sofa and crawled back over to him. "Are *you* okay?" she asked, touching his face tenderly, trying not to hurt him further.

"Yeah, it's fine," Nikos replied, grimacing. "It only hurts a lot."

Anna laughed uncomfortably. "I am *so* sorry, Nikos. I didn't mean to hit you. But thank you for breaking my fall."

"Don't be silly," he said, trying to smile. "I'm the one that tracked in the water."

"This is true. You really only have yourself to blame." They both laughed, though Anna could tell he was hurt.

"Let me call for some ice," she said, using his towel to pat around the area. She wasn't sure she was doing anything helpful, but she kept doing it, anyway, until he grabbed her hand, rubbing his thumb along her palm. She could feel his breath on her wrist, and she was sure he could feel her heart beating out of control.

"No, it's okay, really" he said softly, "I need to get home and get ready anyway."

"You can't drive like this."

"It's okay," he said, "your grandfather should be leaving in a few minutes. I can get him to take me home, and then I'll bring the Vespa back. The wedding is just down the beach from here, so we can walk."

"I don't know," Anna said, "I don't love the idea of you driving like this, especially on a motorbike."

He grabbed her hand and looked her in the eye. "Anna, I'm fine. I'll be careful, I promise."

She nodded, her hand still against his face. "Okay. At least let me help you find Christos." She stood up and pulled him to his feet, only a slight groan escaping him. She could tell he was trying to act tough.

"Seriously Anna, I'm fine," he said as they walked toward the door. "Hey, on the bright side, at least my bruise will match your dress!"

After he left, Anna finished unpacking and started getting ready. She had actually brought almost all of her clothes with her – it was easier to just dump everything into a suitcase than try to guess what she'd want for the next three days – including several dress options, half of them blue. What could she say? Blonde hair, blue eyes... it had been her favorite color to wear since she had watched Cinderella as a kid. She hadn't worn any of them since she'd come to Santorini, sticking mostly to a tank tops and cut-offs uniform. But now it was her chance to get dressed up, and she felt truly giddy at the idea. A couple of the dresses would be hard to wear with a bra, and she wasn't lucky enough to be able to get away without one like some girls, so she put them to the side.

After a few minutes, she settled on the dress she wanted – a structured cotton midi dress with a high neck that she figured would be perfect for a church wedding – and hung it in the bathroom so the creases would fall while she showered. She picked up the bikini wax kit that she had bought at the drug store and tried to decipher the instructions. She wasn't expecting a lot of action *down there* tonight, but it felt incongruous to get all dressed up and not at least put in an effort. The only problem was that she had never used an at-home wax kit, and the instructions were in Greek, making them about as helpful to Anna as an IKEA manual. She considered running down to the bar to ask Elena to translate, but she didn't want her reading into the fact that she was waxing her downstairs to go to a wedding with Nikos. In the end, she decided to stick with shaving.

As Anna got out of the shower, she bent over to wrap

a towel around her hair, but as she stood up she knocked her dress off its hanger and into a puddle of water. "Shit," she muttered, picking it up off the floor. Most of it was completely soaked.

She looked at the time on her phone. She didn't have long enough to finish getting ready and dry her dress, so she put on the bathrobe, went out onto the patio and hung the dress up there, hoping the air would dry it while she finished her hair and makeup. But after she was done, as she came out of the bathroom praying for a miracle, her face fell when she saw that the dress was still dripping on the cement.

With only ten minutes to go until Nikos was due to return, Anna went back to her other pile of dresses. There was only one that looked formal enough for a wedding, but she was going to have trouble with the bra situation. Unless...

Anna dug through the drawer where she had emptied all of her underwear and pulled out what she considered her sexiest bra, though she had never actually worn it. She had bought it when she and Marcus had started dating, but he had bought her far less tasteful, far more expensive lingerie that she had always felt obligated to wear. While it was no surprise that those didn't make the journey, Anna thanked her lucky stars that she had packed this one. It was a white longline lace bra with delicate boning, sheer everywhere else, even on the cups. It was the only strapless bra she had owned that she didn't feel like she had to constantly pull up, and this dress definitely required a strapless bra.

She grabbed a white lace thong to go with it – not that anyone would see it, she told herself – and put them on quickly before grabbing the iron out of the wardrobe. She carefully steamed the creases out of the dress, careful not to get the satin wet, and then slipped it on.

As she looked in the mirror, she felt her stomach flutter. The pale blue dress was clingy and flowy at the same time, hitting all of her curves without being *too* sugges-tive. The delicate straps and V-neck cut showed off the freckles that had started to appear along her shoulders and chest. The slit was just high enough for Anna's leg to peek out without being inappropriate for the church, or at least she hoped. Her strappy heels matched almost perfectly, cutting thin lines across her feet and ankles. The sheer white scarf she had to cover up with in the church was just see-through enough that she could see the silhouette of the dress through it when she wrapped it around her shoulders. Her favorite silver pendant necklace nestled perfectly in the shape of the neckline. She let her hair back down out of its up-do, the waves bouncing across her collarbone, and tried to think of what she could do with it instead. She pulled a sprig of baby's breath from the bouquet on the table and tucked it behind her ear. *Perfect.* She truly felt like a princess on her way to the ball.

When Nikos arrived, his mouth dropped open.

"Anna, you look incredible," he said, scanning her up and down. He lifted her hand and spun her around, her dress billowing as she twirled. "Seriously, you've outdone yourself."

"You don't look so bad yourself," she said, admiring his black tuxedo, trying not to notice too much how the shirt clung to his chest. "Like a Greek James Bond."

Nikos stopped what he was doing and put one hand on his lapel, squinting his eyes. "Stirred, not shaken," he said in a deep voice.

Anna laughed. "Okay, I've never seen a single James Bond film and even I know that's not right."

He shrugged. "Neither have I, in case you couldn't tell from our film night."

Nikos had a small bag of rice tucked under his arm, and Anna grabbed it and turned it over in her hand. "Planning to make a curry later?"

"Very funny," he said, taking it back. "You'll see what it's for."

"Your bruise looks less than ideal." Anna lifted a finger to gently touch the now-purple ring around his eye, and he flinched as she made contact.

"It's fine," he said. "I iced it a bit at home, and once we start drinking, I'm sure it won't hurt to blink anymore."

Anna must have looked mortified, because Nikos instantly apologized, assuring her that it didn't hurt at all. She *almost* believed him.

Anna grabbed her purse from the table, checking to

make sure she had everything she needed. "Shall we get out of here?"

Nikos offered his elbow, and she took it. "We shall."

An hour later, Anna and Nikos walked out of the church into the evening light. The ceremony had been long, as promised, but it was far from boring. Even though it was all in Greek, Anna thought it was beautiful. Nikos had translated under his breath most of the time, telling her the traditions behind each part. For the common cup, he explained how the bride and groom drank from the same cup, taking turns, to symbolize how marriage works, giving and taking, sharing everything. The exchanging of the crowns was also interesting, though Nikos was fuzzy on the reason behind that one. Anna thought it was beautiful, anyway.

But the best part by far had been when the entire audience threw rice at the bride and groom. When Nikos whispered to her what was about to happen, she pictured an American wedding where guests lightly tossed the rice over couples as they left. But this was a completely different animal. Some people threw it as hard as they could, handfuls at a time. A couple of people even ran up to the front and dumped the rice over their heads. After the frenzy had died down, Anna asked why they had done it.

"The Greek word for rice is very similar to the word for root, and the idea is that the more rice is thrown, the more the couple will root together and become one."

As they walked into the hotel where the reception was taking place, Anna and Nikos gasped in unison. The ceiling was completely covered in flowers and foliage, lights twinkling like stars in a canopy of trees. The tables were massive, seating at least twenty people each, and had huge tree trunks growing up through the middle of each one.

"This is amazing," Nikos said. "Weddings are never this extravagant here."

"Really? This is pretty standard for Manhattan," Anna said, "at least from what I've heard. I've never been to one like this though."

"It's funny that you say that. Myrto is actually Greek-American. She's lived in New York since she was a kid."

They walked over to what looked like the table plan. It was a giant slice of a tree trunk, with hundreds and hundreds of rings. Anna guessed it must have come from a massive oak tree, as it was at least four feet across. The names and table numbers looked like they had been individually burned into the tree.

"Someone went all out," Anna whispered as they made their way to their seats. "This must have cost a fortune."

Apparently everyone else felt the same way, because as they sat down, they heard the people at the table behind them having the same conversation. A Greek woman about her mother's age was sitting next to an American woman several years younger.

"Have you ever been to an American wedding?" the American asked.

"No, not really. I had a friend get married in America a long time ago, so we all thought we'd get a big American wedding invite, but his new wife made him get married in a courthouse."

Anna saw Nikos stiffen next to her. She wondered if they were talking about the people she thought they were talking about.

"Well, she sounds like a peach," the American replied.

"Oh, she was," the Greek woman said. "They were divorced a few years later. She'd been having an affair, and when he found out, she accused him of one instead and got him deported. Kept his kids away from him, too."

Anna felt her jaw clench.

"Holy shit. That's terrible," the American said.

"Yeah, well, we all told him not to trust her. She must have been through half a dozen guys during the summer she was here, none of which he knew about. Ignorance is bliss, I guess."

Anna felt a hand on top of hers and realized she had been squeezing her own leg – it was beginning to go numb. She softened her grip under Nikos's touch.

"You need a drink?"

She nodded in response, and Nikos disappeared, reappearing a couple of minutes later with two gin and tonics and a couple of shots.

"Oh god, Nikos, shots?" she said. "I've been through enough tonight."

"Sorry," he said, picking up his shot and tapping hers

with it. "The bride and groom's signature shots are free at the bar, and I already bought you one drink. All this money spent, you would think they could spring for an open bar."

"Signature shots?"

Nikos shrugged. "I guess it's an American thing. I'm not complaining, though."

Reluctantly, Anna lifted the shot and took it, grimacing as it went down, but a few moments later, as her forehead started to relax and her shoulders began to unclench, she was glad she had. "Are there more of those?" she asked, and Nikos pulled two more from behind his glass, smirking at his clever foresight. They took those shots too, and then the bride and groom were announced to cheers and hollering, Anna and Nikos as loud as the rest of them.

It's nothing you didn't already sort of know, Anna told herself. *Well, except that she cheated while she was here. But is cheating habitually worse than cheating once?* Anna wasn't sure. But it drove home the fact that her mother had not only poisoned her against her father in a way he didn't deserve, but she had also managed to exclude her own missteps from the conversation. She had just been trying to save her own ass.

Anna's first instinct was hatred toward her mother, but she checked herself. She had allowed Grace to keep her from her father, and now Giorgos was gone. Could she justify estranging herself from her only remaining parent, no matter what she had done? She wasn't sure she could.

At the moment, though, she just wanted to forget about

the conversation entirely, and whatever revelations it had inspired. She wanted to have fun tonight. And she knew just how to do that.

She kept her glass filled all through dinner, got signature shots for her and Nikos between every course, and pulled him out onto the dance floor the second she could. In her attempt to forget what she'd overheard, Anna managed to truly relax for the first time since she had arrived on the island.

15

As the evening wore on and midnight passed, more and more of the older guests started to leave, and the dance music transitioned from traditional Greek music to the kind of stuff she had heard at the resort bar. Anna and Nikos danced with everyone, saying hello to people they knew as they danced past, but as the hours slipped by they became more and more focused on each other. By the time more guests started to leave, they were pressed together on the dance floor, hips touching, swaying to the beat. Every now and then, Anna would smile at Nikos and feel herself go a bit red in the cheeks, and he would exhale and then chuckle a bit, as if he had dreamed the moment and couldn't believe it was coming true. It felt like a dream to Anna, too. During one song, when the dance floor was mostly full of couples staring even more intensely at each other than Anna and Nikos were, Nikos let out a sigh and stepped back.

"Come on," he said, holding out his hand. "Let's get out of here."

Anna put her hand in his, and they started toward the door. As they walked past the bar, Anna grabbed one of the bottles of champagne from the counter and started to run. Nikos ran alongside her, both of them laughing. She slipped off her heels as they reached the sand, sprinting along the shore toward the resort as if they were being chased. She suspected no one would miss the champagne, but it felt conspiratorial; like they were on the run. It felt exciting. It felt fun.

As they neared the resort, Anna began to shush Nikos. It was well past midnight, and he was singing some song in Greek as they stumbled through the sand. He cheered as they reached the resort, nearly collapsing on a beach chair, and Anna was grateful that the beach was unusually quiet. She sat down behind him and stared out at the darkness.

"Oh my god, I have the best idea," Nikos said, standing up again and beginning to unbutton his shirt. "We are so going for a swim right now."

"No way," Anna said, trying to get him to sit back down. "You're not supposed to swim when you've been drinking. Or at night." But Nikos was already stripping down.

This time he went all the way down to his underwear, and Anna didn't even try not to stare as he walked down the beach toward the water. The faint light from the resort reflected off the sweat glistening on his back, highlighting his muscles. She stood up to follow him, as if he were a magnet.

196

"Come on, we won't go too deep," he said, stepping toward her and putting a hand lightly on either side of her waist. Then, in a whisper, said, "What's the worst that could happen?"

He pulled her closer to him, and Anna felt herself press against him instinctually. She knew exactly what could happen. But whether it was the signature shots or the romance of being on the beach all alone, Anna wasn't sure she cared. She slipped one strap of her dress down over her shoulder, and then the other. Nikos's eyes went wide as she shimmied out of it, revealing the sheer bra she was wearing underneath. He let out a heavy breath. She was all but naked in front of him, and he didn't attempt to disguise how he felt about that. In fact, she could feel it.

Then she ran past him and splashed straight into the ocean.

By the time she turned around, certain that her hair and makeup must be all over the place but laughing anyway, Nikos was wading in behind her. She turned around and smiled at him, half appreciation for him and half appreciation for the way he was clearly appreciating her. She tried to remember all the reasons she hadn't let anything happen with Nikos, but the booze was drowning them at the moment.

She splashed him as he got close, and then he splashed her back. But then he swam slowly up to her, and she didn't step away. As he got closer, he placed his hands gently on her hips and lifted her up until she was wrapped around his waist, pressed close enough together to feel each other's heartbeats. To feel everything.

Anna's breath went shallow as Nikos slowly leaned his head toward hers. She could feel the heat of his breath on her face, the smell of wine just as intoxicating as it had been when they'd been drinking it. He was waiting for her to give him the go-ahead; to tell him that she was okay. *Not too deep*, she told herself, but somehow she knew this would send her right off into the deep end of her feelings. But she couldn't bring herself to care.

With the sea around them and the stars above them and Santorini behind them, Anna pressed her mouth against Nikos's, her head spinning with intoxication of every kind. He kissed her back, soft but firm, his hands running over her back and up her neck. She felt his tongue against hers as their kiss deepened, and she felt herself begin to rock her hips against his. He grabbed her ass and aided her movement, their pace quickening. Anna let out a moan as she felt him begin to react, tilting her head back as he kissed her neck. She ran her hands down his back and slipped them under the waistband of his underwear, ready to throw caution fully to the wind.

And just as she was about to, she heard someone call her name from the shoreline.

"Do you think the lighter grout was the right call?" Anna asked, wiping her forehead and staring down at the off-white grout they were spreading between the tiles.

"Well, I'd say it's a bit late to question that," Elena said, wiping a tile clean. She was right, of course. They were nearly done with the floor, heading toward the front door just like Anna and Nikos had the day before. Of course, this had taken a lot longer. Not only was Nikos not helping, but Anna and Elena had to watch seven different YouTube videos to figure out what they were doing. Plus, they hadn't really gotten started until nearly noon thanks to Anna's killer hangover.

Elena had been walking down the beach with Vasilis after finishing her shift at the bar when she'd seen Anna and Nikos in the ocean. Anna had very quickly snapped out of her lustful haze and after quickly scrambling back into their clothes, Nikos had bid her a hasty goodnight. Anna hadn't seen or spoken to him since then. She knew she should say something; he probably thought she was angry. And she was. But she was angry with herself, not with him.

Now the sun was setting, the two girls had barely spoken all day, and Anna's stomach was rumbling. "Shall we wrap this up and go get some food?" she said, eyeing the last couple of tiles that needed grouting.

"Sure," Elena said, "but I think we should talk first."

Anna nodded and kept working. Elena did the same, the two working in parallel like they had been for most of the afternoon.

"I'm so sorry," Anna started. "I know I shouldn't have let it get that far with Nikos. But we were really drunk. I know it's not an excuse, but it's true. I won't let it happen again. I'll keep my feelings in check."

Elena chuckled softly. "You think I'm angry that you have feelings for Nikos?"

"Well... yeah. Isn't that what's happening here?"

Elena laughed again and stopped scraping, sitting back on her knees. "Not at all, Anna. You're my friend. I think you're great. And I think you and Nikos would be great together."

The two girls stared at each other silently for a moment, Elena smiling and Anna frowning. "I'm confused. Then why did you stop us last night? Not that I'm not grateful, but why?"

"That's why," Elena said. "Because you're grateful. You know deep down that you and Nikos would be good together, but you also think that it's a bad idea. Why is that?"

Anna sighed. "Because I'm leaving."

"Damn right. Because you're leaving. And if you hook up with him and let him get his hopes up and then leave, you're no better than the other girls who come here for their *Sisterhood of the Traveling Pants* romance and then fuck off back to their normal lives. You can sleep with whomever you want. But it would break his heart. And I think that would hurt both of us, wouldn't it?"

Anna couldn't say anything. She could just nod. Elena was completely right. She had judged Nikos for catching feelings for tourists, but she was allowing the same thing to happen now. Except she had a chance to prevent it.

"Unless..." Elena said after Anna didn't respond, "you're considering staying?"

"No, you're right," Anna said, shaking her head. She still hadn't told Elena about the gallery placement, but she also didn't want them to think she was sticking around. "I do care about him. But I am leaving. And that's why I can't let anything happen."

Elena stood up and stepped over to Anna. "I really like you, Anna. I consider you a friend. But my loyalty is to Nikos. I'd love to know that we could be friends without me feeling like I'm betraying my family or letting him get hurt."

Anna reached out to take Elena's hand, and Elena pulled

her to her feet. "I promise," Anna said. "I won't do anything to hurt him."

Just as they were finishing up, Anna heard the truck pull up outside, and she heard Christos and Nikos chatting. Anna locked the door to the summer house and followed Elena out through the gate.

"All done, girls?" Nikos asked casually, but he didn't make eye contact with Anna.

"Yep, all done," Elena said. "You driving us back?"

Nikos nodded and said something to Christos, who responded and threw him the keys. Finally, Nikos looked at Anna, and his face softened. "Christos wants to know if we all want to come over for lunch on Monday. It's a public holiday."

Anna looked at Christos and gave him a thumbs-up. He returned it with both hands and a huge smile on his face.

"I'll go in the back," Elena said, hopping into the bed of the truck. Anna felt her cheeks go red as Nikos opened the passenger door and looked at her.

"Shall we?" he said with a sigh.

Anna climbed in with a feeble smile, and Nikos walked around and got in the driver's seat. As he turned on the ignition and started down the drive, Anna looked behind her to make sure Elena wasn't listening, but she had headphones in.

"Listen, Nikos, about last night—"

"Don't say a thing," he said. "It was completely my fault."

"I mean, it wasn't," Anna said. "I have as much to apologize for as you do."

"No way," he said. "I came onto you, and it was wrong. You asked me not to, and I went against that."

Anna considered this for a moment, but it was annoying her for some reason. She couldn't help but say something. "I never asked you not to come onto me," she said. "I told you I didn't want anything to happen."

"Same thing, isn't it?"

"Not really, no." Nikos looked at her, confused. "I think it's an important distinction. If I had actually asked you not to do anything, then most of our relationship would be in violation of that. But I didn't say that. I just said I didn't want anything to happen. And anything that has happened has been just as much my doing as it has been yours."

"Okay," Nikos said, "but it still feels like I'm the one who owes you an apology."

"I don't agree," Anna said. "I don't feel like either of us did anything wrong. It was just a kiss. I just think we need to be clear about the page we're on. Make sure we're on the same one."

"And what page is that?"

Anna thought about this for a moment. As much as she didn't want to hurt him, she hadn't felt in the wrong last night. It had felt good. But as she looked over at Nikos, she knew that the best thing for him was for them to stay friends. *Just* friends. And if she cared about his feelings, then that was the best thing for her, too.

"I think we're on the friendship page. And while we briefly turned that page last night, I don't think we passed the point of no return."

Nikos sighed. "If you say so."

"What do you mean?"

He pressed his lips together and looked from the road to Anna and back to the road, back and forth, like he wasn't sure he should say what was on his mind.

"I mean that you seem to want to get together," he said. Anna felt herself go red again, and it didn't go unnoticed. "See? You're even blushing. I just don't understand why you keep insisting that it would be a bad thing." He reached over to the passenger seat and put his hand on her thigh, rubbing it with his thumb. His touch felt so good, and Anna immediately slipped back into last night; into the desire to just give in to what she was feeling. But without the booze to drown her concerns, and with the light of day shining on them, she couldn't ignore the truth.

"Because I don't want to just *get together*, Nikos," she said, her voice raised. "I care too much about you. And I don't want either of us to get hurt when I leave."

Nikos pulled his hand back, placing it back on the steering wheel. "Well, that sucks," he says. "But I guess it's nice to know that it's not all in my head."

Anna looked at him and tried to smile, but she knew it wasn't quite convincing. "Of course it's not in your head."

He nodded. "Thanks for being honest... I guess. But can I just say one thing?" The truck pulled past the sign for the resort, and Nikos guided it into one of the service spots, turning off the engine. Elena climbed out of the back and started walking toward the building.

"Sure."

"I'm going to be hurt when you leave no matter what. Even if we never get together. I care about you, too. And I'm going to be sad to lose you when you go."

He leaned across and kissed Anna lightly on the cheek, then got out of the truck and went inside, leaving Anna alone with her thoughts.

When she finally made her way inside, she found Elena and Nikos sitting on the sofa in her room with Xenia, who was showing Elena how to control the lighting, dimming the sconces next to the bed.

"Hi, Xenia," she said when she walked in. "You alright?"

"Yeah, great," she replied. "I just wanted to check in and see how the new room was."

"It's amazing," Anna said.

"Yeah, she especially loves the sea views," Elena said, and both Anna and Nikos glared at her.

"I'm not even going to ask," Xenia said with a laugh. "But no issues so far?"

Anna scanned the room quickly, trying to remember anything she'd noticed. "Nothing that doesn't work, but I thought it could be nice to have shaving plug adapters for the bathroom. Since there's a vanity in there, it would be great to be able to use hair dryers, straighteners, stuff like that."

Xenia nodded. "I'll have to see if there are any safety rules about that, but I like the suggestion."

Elena picked Anna's camera up off the coffee table and waved it at Anna. "Ooh, can we look at pictures of me, please?"

"What's this?" Xenia asked.

"I had a little photoshoot with Elena the other day," Anna said, pulling the memory card out and putting it into the USB adapter.

"Oh, this I've got to see." Xenia sat down on the sofa next to Nikos. "You should be able to plug that directly into the TV."

Anna reached around and plugged in the USB. Nikos turned on the TV with the remote and they started scrolling through the pictures, starting with the ones of just Elena, then through the ones of the girls who had paid Anna, and, finally, through the ones of Elena and Vasilis.

"Who is that?" Xenia asked. "You two seem to be getting along quite well."

"His name's Vasilis. He's visiting his aunt for the summer. You know, Kassandra?"

"Oh yeah, I knew she had a nephew visiting from Athens, but I thought he was like seven!"

"Try twenty-seven," Elena said, smiling. "We've been together almost every night since."

Anna looked at Elena. "I didn't know that! You really like him, then?"

"Well, you've been a little busy," Elena said, nudging her. "Plus, didn't you hear us talking all through the photo-shoot?"

"You were speaking Greek. He could have been teaching you physics, for all I knew."

The others laughed. "Well, we really like each other," Elena said. "Sometimes that's enough."

Anna tried not to feel like Elena was being pointed, focusing instead on flipping through the rest of the photos. She went through the one of Nikos down at the harbor, and then she was into the photos she had taken of the room the previous day.

"Oh my god," Xenia said, staring at the screen.

"What?" Anna asked. "What's wrong?"

"Nothing. These are incredible." Xenia looked at Anna. "Did you take these on this camera?"

Anna nodded.

"I had a professional come in a couple of days ago who brought tons of expensive equipment with him, and he couldn't get a shot even half as good as these."

"Oh, well, I can send them to you if you'd like," Anna said. "Feel free to use them."

"I have a better idea. How about I pay you to come take more of them?"

Anna's jaw dropped. "*Seriously?*"

"Yes, *seriously*. These pictures are exactly what I was

looking for for the new website and marketing campaign. But we would have to do it really soon. Like, tomorrow."

"I would love that," Anna said without hesitation. "Let's do it."

"Amazing." Xenia stood up from the sofa and shook Anna's hand. "I'll come by tomorrow while you're on your shift at the cafe and we can talk about it." Then she walked out of the room, closing the door behind her.

Take that, Marcus, she thought. This was everything she could hope for. Someone else actually wanted to pay her for her work, and knowing this made her feel better than she ever had before. Maybe she didn't need to rely on Marcus for success after all.

"Oh my god, Anna!" Elena shouted, standing up and wrapping her in a hug. "Congratulations! That's amazing!"

Nikos caught Anna's eye. "I told you you're talented," he said, joining the group hug for a moment. "Why don't I go get us some pizza to celebrate? Alfresco should be open."

"That sounds so good right now," Elena said, pulling away. "Could you?"

"Anything for the professional photographer," Nikos said, grabbing the keys to the truck.

"This is so exciting!" Elena said after he left. "Are you absolutely buzzing right now?"

"Yeah, basically," Anna said. It was a feeling she couldn't compare to anything else she'd felt. She was being paid to do the thing she loved. First the girls in Oia, and now

Xenia. "Oh, shit," she said, "I just realized I still haven't sent those girls their photos yet."

"Well, we can't have that," Elena said, "you've got a reputation to uphold. Let's get to it."

They sat down at Anna's computer, moving the memory card over and choosing the best photos. In the end, Anna sent over forty photos to each girl, trying to make sure they had plenty of poses and locations to choose from.

"Look at you, getting paid to take photos. That's exactly what you said you wanted to do!" Elena held her hand out in front of Anna, who high-fived her.

"I know," Anna said, shutting her laptop and turning to face her friend. "I just didn't expect it to happen so fast."

"That's the thing. If you do something enough and you're good at it, people will notice. You probably are getting all this opportunity because you weren't *trying* to be a photographer. You were just *being* one."

"That's incredibly wise," Anna said. "You're like Obi Wan Kenobi or Oprah or something." She remembered the bottle of champagne she had stolen from the wedding the night before. "Should we celebrate? I have some champagne in the fridge."

"Yes!" Elena shouted in response, jumping up and grabbing the bottle from the fridge, immediately working on the foil. "Xenia must really like you."

"Actually, that's from the wedding last night," Anna admitted. "We stole it when we came back here. Turns out we didn't need it."

Elena laughed. "Probably for the best. You would have drowned if you had been any more intoxicated than you were last night."

"That's what I said to Nikos." Anna flinched as Elena popped the cork, then reached out her hand to accept a glass after Elena had filled them.

"We should probably finish this before Nikos comes back," Elena said. "There are only two glasses, and I am *not* sharing."

Anna laughed and nodded, taking a big sip of her champagne. At least Elena wasn't angry with her.

They didn't quite manage to finish the bottle before Nikos got back, but it turned out to be a good thing since he had a case of beer with him, along with another bottle of sparkling wine.

"I see you guys started celebrating without me," he said, setting the pizza and beer down on the table. "Is that the champagne from the wedding?"

"Sure is," Anna said, opening the pizza box. "But the real question is, why did you only get one pizza?"

The rest of the evening, Anna, Elena and Nikos drank beer, ate pizza and room service desserts and watched movies in Anna's bed. At around two, the three of them passed out on the bed, draped over each other like kids at a sleepover. Anna woke up a bit later to use the bathroom, and on her way back she paused and smiled as she looked at the two cousins asleep on either side of the bed. She was glad she had gotten a redo tonight. She needed to know that it was possible to be friends with Nikos and Elena after everything that happened.

As she curled up on the couch under a blanket, she thought about the job Xenia had offered her. Eighteen months as a gallery assistant in Manhattan and she had only ever stared at photos hanging on walls. Now she was going to get to take them. They probably wouldn't end up in a gallery anywhere, but she felt like she was finally a real photographer. Maybe Nikos was right. Maybe she could build a life here.

The second she had that thought, her stomach dropped. It wasn't the plan. She couldn't stay in Santorini forever...

...could she?

Grace,

Today is Lizzy's sixteenth birthday, and all I can do is imagine what she looks like. I can't believe that I don't know what she looks like now. The thought breaks my heart.

If I'm being honest, I've been thinking a lot lately about how we should have done things differently. What's worse, having children you adore and then losing them, or never having them at all? I would obviously never wish Lizzy's and Anna's existences away, but I've definitely fantasized about what it would be like to not carry the pain of what I've been through.

What I really wish is that you hadn't pretended.

You pretended to be in love with me the entire time you were here. I may have been blinded by love, but you never did a thing to help me see clearly. Instead, you made promises to me and plans with me. We had our entire future mapped out, Grace. I still remember perfectly that time we went out on the boat and you said you wanted to open a store in Oia. You would use your law school money to buy one of the buildings. You would open a clothing store on the ground floor and fix up the upstairs to rent out to tourists. You weren't a tourist, you'd say; you were there for good, so you weren't like them. You were going to marry me in the big yellow church down the road and have babies with me and learn to drive stick shift so we could share the car.

And you know what? I think that some part of you actually wanted those things. Not with me, necessarily, but I think you were longing to be that person. You wanted to be carefree and unambitious and content with a simple life. The problem was that you never truly were. And I was so busy falling in love with the person you pretended to be that I never saw who you really were.

I don't blame you for that. But I don't blame myself anymore, either. You were always going to be the kind of person to leave, and I was always going to follow. Not to sound like a fatalist, but I can't imagine the situation playing out any other way. I just hate that it did. And eight years later, I still cry almost every day because of what you took away from me. What my ignorance to the real you ended up costing me. On the best days, I'm heartbroken. On the worst days, I wish none of it had ever happened.

I know you probably won't, but I have to ask. I will always ask. Could I please see them? Could I please speak to my children? Could you at least tell them that I love them?

No, I didn't think so.

Giorgos

17

"These look incredible," Elena said. "I can't believe you were able to get these shots given how dark it was outside."

Eirini motioned for the camera, and Elena handed it to her. She held it up, leaning back so she could see the photo displayed on the screen.

"Very nice," she said, handing the camera back to Anna. "You should be very proud."

"It's amazing what a reflector and the right settings can do," Anna said.

"It's amazing what the right photographer can do," Elena replied. She smiled at Anna across the table.

They were sat out on the patio enjoying the sunshine after yesterday's scattered showers. Anna had finally experienced bad weather in Greece, and of course it had to happen on the same day as her photoshoot at the resort. Xenia had even given Elena the day off specially to help, despite it being the first day of the holiday weekend. Xenia suggested postponing until after the launch, but Anna insisted on trying, which turned out to be the right decision. The cloudy skies ended up adding a moodiness to the photos that went perfectly with the sleek new website design Xenia had showed her, and it meant she didn't have to worry about bright direct light. The rain had held off just long enough to finish the exterior shots. The interiors would need a bit of editing magic to brighten them up, but it was nothing Anna couldn't handle.

"Thanks for your help," she said to Elena, who had spent the day holding the reflector and making adjustments as needed.

"No problem. You can send my fee along any time," she replied, winking.

"Let me go see what's taking your grandfather so long with the mezze," Eirini said, standing and heading inside.

"I am absolutely starving," Anna said, closing her eyes as she sat back and tilted her face toward the sun.

The island had been absolutely crawling all weekend for *Agiou Pnevmatos*, a national public holiday. In other words, as Anna now knew, the entire mainland of Greece emptied to the islands, even as far south as Santorini. So she and Elena had spent all weekend in the cafe, listening to Xenia shout last-minute orders at people as things came up that hadn't been finished before the opening. Meanwhile, Nikos spent his time painting the summer house. Anna insisted that he didn't need to, that he could wait until she was off work, but he had insisted.

They still hadn't spoken any more about what had happened between them, but Anna was okay with that. He wasn't acting weird toward her, so she didn't want to rock the boat. After all, this is what she'd wanted, right? So what good would come from discussing it?

"How was your date last night?" Anna asked Elena.

"So good," she said. "Vasilis is seriously so hot. Everything he does is sexy. Picks me up on his actual motorcycle? Sexy. Orders the vegetarian dish? Sexy. Always offers to go down on me? Sexy."

"Gross!" Anna shouted, throwing a napkin at Elena. "I *so* didn't need to know that."

"Whatever," Elena replied, throwing the napkin back at her. "You're just salty because I cock-blocked you after the wedding."

"I mean, I'm not *happy* that I haven't gotten laid in over a month," Anna said. "It's the longest I've gone in a while."

Elena sat up and hit Anna's arm lightly. "Oh my god, did you have a boyfriend before you came here? That would explain so much!"

"Not exactly..." Anna started. Then, "Wait, what would that explain?"

Elena shrugged. "Why you're so desperate to get back."

"I'm not *desperate* to get back. I just know it's the best thing for everyone."

"Whatever. Agree to disagree. But back to the guy."

"Right. The guy." Anna hadn't thought much about Marcus since she arrived. Not in that way, anyway. Not even when he had emailed her about the contest. He had turned out to be as forgettable to her as she seemed to be to him. "I was casually seeing this guy for just over a year back home."

"How often did you sleep with him?"

Anna thought back to her time with Marcus, remembering the texts he would send giving her a day, time and place. Never any asking. No discussion. Just a when and where. And she always went. "A couple of times a week," she said. "He had a busy schedule."

"Um, excuse me, a year of seeing each other every few days isn't exactly casual."

"Yeah, well, it was a weird circumstance."

"Define weird."

Anna hesitated, but she couldn't think of a reason not to tell Elena the truth. "He was my boss."

"Oh, shit, girl! That's so shady."

"Not really," she said. "It wasn't like that. I never felt like he was hanging it over my head until the end, when I quit my job to come here. He didn't like me bringing up our history to get what I wanted."

"What did he do?"

"He fired me, actually."

Elena shrugged. "It kind of sounds like it was 'like that,'" she said, making air quotes with her hands.

"Yeah, well, it wasn't."

"So he didn't buy you expensive gifts that no one else would ever see, like lingerie or something? And he didn't sneak you around, always having you over to his, never to yours? He didn't call you 'cute' when you showed him things you were excited about? He didn't sleep with other women and then try to make you feel crazy for not being okay with it?"

Good point, Anna thought, remembering the time she showed Marcus the picture she had taken of a lighthouse on Long Island. He had actually used the word "cute."

"Okay, maybe it was a little bit *like that*."

Elena threw her head back and laughed. "It's alright, girl. We all need a little bit of that to learn from."

"You sound like you know," Anna replied, chuckling.

Just then, Nikos came through the gate, and Anna sat up a bit straighter. She wasn't sure why, but she didn't want to talk about Marcus in front of him. She may not have done anything wrong, but she also wasn't particularly proud of their relationship.

Eirini and Christos followed soon after, each with a plate of mezze in each hand.

"It looks so good in there," Eirini said, setting down plates in front of them. The three of them immediately dug in. "Nikos was just showing us around."

"Thank you," Anna said between bites. "He's been working really hard on it this weekend."

"It's all Giorgos's plans," Nikos said with his mouth full, earning a nasty look from Eirini.

While she'd kept the inside of the summer house a traditional white, Anna had decided to follow Giorgos's plan to paint the outside a vibrant yellow. She had also used the money from the girls in town to buy shutters and window boxes to turn it into a little cottage. Now all it needed was flowers trailing out of the boxes. Oh, and the dozens of other things on Anna's list.

She and Elena had spent the morning helping Nikos finish the inside, which was now looking clean and bright. The terracotta tiles looked beautiful with the white walls and cabinets and big picture windows. Nikos and Kostas had even managed to hunt down enough of the materials for the backsplash Giorgos had sketched in his notes: gorgeous blue, white and terracotta patchwork tiles that tied the whole room together. The new countertops were a lovely piece of natural wood that had been imported from Athens; a costly purchase using most of Anna's advance from Xenia, but worth it. Giorgos's vision for the summer house was coming together, and the closer they got to accomplishing it, the better Anna felt. That afternoon they were bringing in the new cabinet fronts, and next week, when they brought the appliances from Nikos's, the kitchen would be done.

"Well, I for one love seeing it come to life," Eirini said. "It's been long enough since that place saw any kind of hope."

Since your mother came and ruined everything, everyone finished in their heads. At least, Anna imagined that they did. She certainly did. If reading her father's letters had taught her anything, it was that her father was much better off before her mother came along.

"House looks good," Christos added with a big grin, clearly proud of himself for stringing so many words together. Anna laughed and reached across the table to touch his hand. Her grandparents had been so supportive, even after realizing she was planning to sell the house. She had definitely lucked out where they were concerned.

Anna's phone buzzed, and she picked it up off the table to check the notification.

"Anna!" Christos shouted, shaking his head. "No phone while eat."

"Sorry," Anna said, "it's for work."

"Elena says you've had some more work come through, Anna?" Eirini asked.

"Yes, I do," she said. "I have the work at the hotel this week, some shoots in the mornings, and then I'm shooting a wedding next weekend."

As it turned out, one of the girls, the one who had tried to pay her more, the one with the southern accent, had over half a million followers on Instagram. She'd given Anna credit for the photos as she posted them, and suddenly requests had flooded into her inbox from people wanting her to take photos of them on their vacations. One message had been from a bride coming all the way from Chicago to get married on the island, saying her photographer had to cancel at the last minute, offering to pay Anna nearly two thousand euros to photograph her wedding.

"A wedding! How lovely." Eirini said, clapping her hands together.

"Yeah, I'm excited but nervous," Anna said. "It's such an important day for them, especially the bride. I would hate to mess it up."

"You won't," Nikos said. "I've seen your photos. No one has an eye like you do. It's really something special."

"Thank you," Anna replied, smiling affectionately. Nikos returned her smile before turning back to his meal. It was a perfectly friendly exchange – intimate even, in its own way – but it rang hollow after the loaded glances and intense gazing of the last three and a half weeks.

"Do you know what this holiday is?" Eirini asked, smiling and looking around, hoping she'd stumped them.

"*Agiou Pnevmatos*," Elena answered. "Monday of the Holy Spirit."

"Yes, but do you know what it means?"

Nikos and Elena hung their heads, clearly embarrassed that they didn't know what it was. Eirini and Christos weren't particularly religious, but they at least knew their holidays.

"It's the day the Holy Spirit was given to the followers of Christ," she said, sounding like a teacher giving a lecture.

Anna nodded. "That's interesting."

"Why is it interesting, dear?"

Anna's eyes went wide as she looked to Nikos and Elena

for help. Very *un*helpfully, they started giggling. "Um, I don't really know."

"Well, then, best to let me finish," Eirini said, winking at her. "It's interesting because it was on this day, fifty days after Easter, that the Trinity was complete. Father, Son, and Holy Spirit."

Eirini looked at Anna, but she had learned her lesson. She kept her mouth shut. Eirini turned to Nikos and Elena.

"Now, I've watched you two be each other's best friends since you were little. This is a small island, and you two have been through enough for everyone on it. But Anna here has completed your trinity. And while she isn't staying forever, it's been so nice to see all three of you so happy."

Elena reached across the table and grabbed Anna's hand. Anna squeezed, and Elena squeezed back. Nikos took Elena's other hand, and after a moment of hesitation reached out for Anna's hand as well.

"That's beautiful," Anna said. "Thank you for saying that."

She looked across the table at her two friends. She had been with them for such a short time, but she already considered them some of the best friends she had ever had. And it hurt her to think what she would do without them.

After they had finished their meals and Elena left to go meet Vasilis, Anna and Nikos went back to the summer house.

"It really does look amazing in here," Nikos said, looking around as he reached into the refrigerator for a beer. He handed one to Anna.

"Thanks," she said. "Yeah, it really does. I thought I knew what I wanted to do, but it turns out my dad knew best. Which makes sense since he built the place."

Nikos laughed softly, and Anna cocked her head at him.

"It's just that that's the first time you've called him your dad," he said, smiling. He sat down at the table. "It's nice to hear."

Anna joined him at the table and twisted open her beer, taking a big sip. "Well, the more I read his letters, the more I realize how much my mother lied. About him, about this place... all of it. So if I'm going to know the truth about him, I have to let go of all that. And my anger toward him, the hatred that was keeping me from acknowledging him as my father, was based on a lie."

Nikos nodded. "That seems like a lot."

"Yeah, but being here helps," she replied. "Being with you and with his parents – it all helps. I feel like I know him more through you. Through all of this." She paused for a moment. "Lizzy told me what he did for you, you know. Sending you to college. Forcing you to stay there. And what you did for him, coming back."

"He was the closest thing to a father I've ever had," Nikos said. "It was an easy decision."

"But why did you stay here?" she asked. "Why didn't

you go somewhere else? Surely, you could get a job anywhere."

He shrugged. "I didn't want to. I like it here."

"But when you could go anywhere in the world?"

Nikos sighed and leaned forward, propping his elbows up on his knees. "London wasn't great for me if I'm being honest. The school was, but not the place. Not the environment. I didn't like who I became. When I came home, I felt like myself again. Like my priorities were realigned. Sometimes you have to leave home to know how much you miss it, ya know?"

Anna nodded while she was listening, but at his question she stopped and shook her head. "Honestly? No, I don't. I've never felt that about a place. Not about Connecticut. Not about Manhattan." *Not about here*, she didn't say. Especially as she wasn't sure it was true.

"Well, that's a real shame," Nikos said. "I hope you get to feel it someday."

"Me too."

Later that evening, after the new cabinets had been installed, Anna and Nikos wandered down to the resort. After weeks of seeing it practically empty, it was weird to see it filled with so many people. It was buzzing with excitement; Xenia had been pushing people for weeks so it would be open for the long weekend, and it seemed like the staff was just as high on the energy as the guests were. They made their way to the beachfront bar where Elena worked, scanning the crowd for her and Vasilis. Which was hard, since it was more people in one place than Anna had seen on the island yet, including a Sunday morning in Oia.

"Just look for the tangled mess of limbs," Anna said, "hers thin, his bulging with muscle."

Sure enough, they found them making out against the bar. Nikos cleared his throat as they approached.

"Oh, hi guys," Elena said as she pulled away. "Have a good afternoon?"

Anna nodded. "I take it you did, too?"

"It was great," Elena said. "I saw Vasilis's aunt Kassandra, and she asked me to lunch tomorrow."

"Wow," Anna said, "someone's moving quickly. Meeting the family already?"

"Well, you know," Elena replied, pulling Vasilis closer to her, "I had already met her on my own, so it made sense. And when you find a good one, you hold on tight."

As they began to kiss again, Anna threw up a hand to try to catch the bartender's attention. "Alright, I think I'm going to need a few more drinks in me if I'm going to watch the two of you all night."

"Yeah, and I'm going to need a sick bag," Nikos said. Elena laughed as Anna ordered a round of drinks.

"Don't listen to these bitter people, baby," she said to Vasilis. Then, to Anna, "His English isn't great, but he promised me he'd try around you so you don't feel left out."

"That's sweet," Anna said. "Thank you."

Vasilis grabbed Elena around the waist and dipped her backward, kissing her like they were in an old Hollywood film. Then he put an arm around her shoulders and kissed her head. "Because today went so good, I could start saying you my girlfriend."

"Are you serious?" she asked, her grin so wide that Anna thought it might split her face in two. And then she started sputtering in Greek, kissing Vasilis every few seconds.

"I take it she said yes?" Anna whispered to Nikos.

"Yep, she sure did."

The bartender set their drinks down, and Anna handed him a note. Nikos picked one up and downed it in about three seconds.

"You alright there?" Anna asked, sipping at hers.

"Great," Nikos said, "just great." Then he picked up another one of the drinks and started on it, too, before Anna grabbed it out of his hand.

"Alright, Amy Winehouse, I think that's good," she said. "What's wrong?"

He flipped his hand in Elena and Vasilis's general direction. "They catch feelings for someone after a week and get a relationship out of it. I do it and... well, let's just say it doesn't usually work like that."

Anna nodded, unsure if she should pretend not to know what he was talking about. But she did understand how he felt. Elena was making bold moves and being rewarded for it. That day in Oia, they had both been standing on a precipice. Elena had decided to jump and figure it out on the way down. Anna, on the other hand, held herself back because she didn't have a parachute. She may have literally jumped that day, but she had been holding herself back. She couldn't shake the envy she felt for Elena. Not because of the muscly man in her arms, but because of the fact that she was in someone's arms at all. Meanwhile Anna stood an appropriate distance away from Nikos, sipping her drink while she watched the party around her.

And even as she realized this, she told herself she was doing the right thing. Elena was being foolish. Vasilis lived all the way in Athens. Would she ask him to stay? Would she be heartbroken if he said no? What would happen when he went back? Not to mention what had happened between her parents. They were the perfect example of "jump now, think later," and that had turned out horribly for everyone. Sure, she wouldn't have existed, but maybe everyone else would have been better off if they had been a bit more cautious and honest with themselves. Maybe her dad would even still be alive.

You're doing the right thing for everyone, she told herself. And most of her believed it.

"Let's dance," she said to Elena, pulling her out of her post-commitment stupor. She dragged her to the middle of the throng, where the people were pressed so close together that no one was really dancing with any one other person. They were all dancing together.

"Congratulations!" Anna shouted at Elena.

"Thanks!" she replied with a thumbs up. "Nikos doesn't look happy." She put on an over-exaggerated frown.

"My fault," Anna said, shrugging her shoulders. They were talking in the way people only do when they can't hear each other: in short phrases and charades.

Elena shook her head. "Not your fault. His fault."

Anna shrugged again, more sincerely this time. She wasn't so convinced of that. But there wasn't anything she could do about it. Nothing she could do in good conscience, anyway. So, instead, she just danced with her friend and three hundred other people, celebrating being a complete trinity, at least for now.

A nna set the plates on the table as Nikos stirred the soup, swaying back and forth to the beat of the song that was playing over the speaker he had brought with him. "You have to be nice to him," she said. "He hasn't done anything wrong."

"When was I not nice?"

"Um, I don't know, maybe when you implied that he was a gold digger because Elena owned the house?"

Nikos laughed. "Oh, yeah. I forgot about that."

Elena had been bringing Vasilis around more and more the past couple of weeks, trying to integrate him into the group. They had learned that he may not speak English, but he was a very highly sought-after naval consultant, which was why he was able to spend so much time away. He had also been very helpful moving in the new kitchen appliances and mixing the cement for the drive (which they all regretted laying themselves because of how long it took). But still, Nikos hadn't exactly warmed to him. He was playing the protective big brother – or cousin, as it were – very convincingly, and Elena wasn't happy about it.

"I know you think they're moving too fast, but she's happy, and that's all that matters."

"Of course, that's not all that matters," he said. "I'd rather her be seventy per cent happy forever than one hundred per cent happy for the next two weeks until he has to go back to Athens."

"You can't see the future," Anna said, pushing Nikos to the side to get the new napkins from the drawer and tugging at the price tag. "You don't know that she won't be happy in a long- distance relationship. You don't even know if it will stay long distance."

Nikos rolled his eyes. "I guess you're right." He looked at the napkins and took them from Anna to try the tag. "Did you just get these?"

"Yeah, I picked them up at a shop in Kamari while I was looking at motorbikes."

Nikos whipped his head up. "You were looking at motorbikes?"

"Yeah," Anna said, taking the liberated napkins from his hands. "Walking to and from work is just taking so much time. With all the photography jobs I'm doing, and a few things still to do around the house, I don't have as much time to spend lumbering up and down the hills as I did when I first got here."

"Isn't that a bit of a waste if you're leaving once the house is done? Buyers aren't exactly going to be worried about the napkins," he said, looking down at what he was cooking.

"Yeah, well, I'm the one living here right now, and I like the napkins. Plus, I don't know how long the house will take to sell. And if I have all of these photography jobs lined up, I might as well stick around until it's sold. It'll certainly be cheaper than paying someone to show it if I've gone."

"Oh, okay," Nikos said, sounding rejected.

Anna realized then what he had really been asking. He had a point. Since Anna had received the email from Marcus, she had kept buying things for the house as if she was staying forever. But the reality was that she had an opportunity for the first time in her life to have the career she had hoped for. She lifted her hand to put it on his arm but then decided against it.

"Nikos, I haven't changed my mind about going. I'm sorry. I would say if I had."

"Oh, that's not what I meant," he said unconvincingly. "But remind me why that is?"

"Because this isn't my life," she said. "I want to be a photographer."

"But you are a photographer. You're doing that now. You can only afford a motorbike and flowers and a new sofa because of all the work you've booked."

"Yeah, but I mean a *real* photographer, not taking photos for wannabe influencers and hotel websites." *The kind who has their work shown in MarMac.*

As soon as the words had come out of her mouth, she wished she could put them back. She didn't know where the snobbery had come from, but there it was, laid out in front of Nikos in all its glory. He turned around slowly, leaning against the counter and crossing his arms.

"So that's what we are to you? A pretend life? Something to bide the time until your real life starts?"

"That's not what I meant—"

"See, I think that's exactly what you meant." His voice was raised now. "You may not have wanted to come here at first, but you're just like all those other girls who come to Santorini for a suntan and a summer fling, consequences be damned. You're just getting a house out if it."

"That's bullshit!" she shouted. "All I do is think about the consequences. What it would mean to take my father's house. What his letters mean. How they affect me and what I've grown up believing. What would happen if I stayed or if I went." *What it would mean to accept Marcus's offer. What it would mean to turn it down. What would happen if I stayed forever. What would happen if I gave into my feelings for you.*

"That's your problem, Anna. It's all about you. But I'm my own person with my own feelings and desires. You need to own up to the fact that it's not concern for me. It's concern for you. For what it would mean for you to give in to your life here. You're scared that you might actually love it. That you might love *me*. And since life here doesn't count as real life in your mind, that scares the shit out of you."

234

He lowered his voice as he continued. "But let me tell you something, Anna. My life here is as real as it gets. You may not understand why I didn't move to a big city and get a fancy job making lots of money, but I do. I work hard every day. I have friends and family I care about. And I love my life here. I was a shell of myself when I was in London. Here, I'm exactly who I want to be. And I think if you were being honest with yourself you would see that you are, too. You're happy here. And just because people come here on vacation doesn't make that happiness any less real."

As Nikos spoke, Anna felt tears forming in her eyes. She tried to fight them back, but as he stopped talking, she felt them start to fall down her cheeks.

"I'm sorry to upset you," he said. "But I'm not sorry for what I said. I really believe it."

Anna stood there with tears trickling down her cheeks for a few seconds, half of her wanting Nikos to come comfort her and half of her wanting to run all the way down the mountain and into the sea. But before her fight-or-flight response could fully kick in, there was a knock at the door.

"Let them in, please," Anna said, heading for the bathroom. "I'll be out in a few minutes." Then she locked herself in the bathroom, sat down in the tub and sobbed.

"This soup is so good," Elena said. "I'm so sick of bar food for dinner. Thanks for having us over."

235

"No problem," Anna said, "though I can't take credit. Nikos made it."

When Elena and Vasilis had arrived, Anna had heard Nikos tell them that she was getting ready in the bathroom. She was grateful for the time he had bought her and used all of it trying to calm herself down.

"Nikos is wrong," she had said in the mirror. "This isn't real life. Not yours, anyway." Probably out of necessity, she had actually believed it for a moment, but as she sat at the table with the people she now realized were her two best friends in the world, she questioned if maybe he was right after all. She felt like she was having an out-of-body experience, not quite able to join in the conversation.

Vasilis started to say something to Nikos in Greek, but Elena cleared her throat, nodding at Anna.

"Oh, sorry, Anna," he said. Then, to Elena, "I don't know how to say it. You say about Maria?"

"Of course, dear," she said, giving him a peck on the cheek. "Vasilis's cousin Maria is coming to live here next week. She works for a winemaker on the mainland who just bought a few vineyards here, and they want her to come manage them."

"That's amazing," Nikos said. "There are so many good ones around here. I bet that's a great job."

"Also," Vasilis said to Nikos, "she see you in Facebook. Wants to meet you."

Anna felt her stomach drop.

"She wants to meet me?" Nikos repeated. "Why?"

"For a…" Vasilis tried, unable to place the word. "*Rantevoú*."

Anna nearly dropped her spoon. "She wants to date me?" Nikos asked.

"Just to meet you," Elena said. "She thinks you're cute, apparently." Anna didn't look up from her bowl, but she could tell Elena was looking at her. Nikos, too, for that matter. Poor Vasilis was the only one who didn't seem to notice how flushed her face was getting. At least not for a moment. But even he eventually realized what the other two were looking at.

"Oh, so sorry, you are boyfriend and girlfriend?" he asked, pointing between Anna and Nikos. The table was silent for a moment.

"No, we're not," Anna finally said, looking up at Vasilis, determined not to lose it at the table.

Nikos looked at Anna, and she could see the wheels turning. Then he nodded almost imperceptibly as he came to a decision. He turned back to Vasilis. "Yeah, okay. Set us up."

At that moment, both Elena and Nikos looked at Anna, and she felt her face go red. She needed to get up before she started crying. Or hyperventilating. Or both.

"You and Maria sound like a great match. Now if you'll excuse me, I need to go check on something outside." Anna pushed her chair back and stood up from the table, walking out the front door just as tears began to fall.

"You've been doing a lot of that tonight," Elena said from behind her a few minutes later.

"Doing what?" she asked without turning around.

"Crying."

So the music hadn't masked her sobs like she had hoped. Not now, and not when they arrived. Oh well. She had caused enough of a scene back there that it was pretty obvious how she felt.

"I'm sorry," she said to Elena. "I didn't mean to ruin dinner."

"I told him not to bring it up," Elena said, putting an arm around Anna. "But, girl, you have to be okay with this. You made your decision, and now you're the one dragging things out. You can't expect Nikos to hold off on living his life until you leave."

"I know. It's just hard."

"It was always going to be. From the moment you two met, it was always going to be a hard goodbye."

They stared out at the hills for a while. The moon was so bright that they could see the waves rolling in toward Kamari beach. The tide was rising, and Anna could imagine the water getting higher and higher, swallowing the resort and the roads and the summer house and all of them in it, and then the whole island. Like a new Atlantis. It seemed more plausible than getting out the other side of this without hurting someone.

"Maybe I don't want to say goodbye," Anna said, turning to her friend. It was terrifying to admit out loud, but Nikos had been right. She knew that. "Maybe this is what I want."

Elena sighed and cupped Anna's face with her hands,

meeting her gaze and holding it. "Then you need to make up your mind."

Grace Linton sighed into the phone, and Anna rolled her eyes. She was sure Lizzy was doing the same thing.

"Don't be ridiculous, Anna. You cannot stay in Greece forever. You have responsibilities here."

"Do I?" Anna asked. "Like what? Because the only thing I can think of is my car that's still at your house, which I haven't actually driven since I moved to Manhattan." She still hadn't told them about the gallery placement, but with everything else she had going on with her photography, it seemed less important.

"Oh, please, I scrapped that last year."

"You scrapped my car?"

"It was a piece of junk, and you seemed perfectly happy in Manhattan. When it was clear you weren't moving back to Connecticut, I got rid of it."

"Well, maybe you should have talked to her about it first." Lizzy interjected.

Anna took a deep breath. "It doesn't matter now. You're actually proving my point. I don't really have anything tying me to the States. I have more here than I do anywhere else."

"She's not wrong, Mom," Lizzy said. "She's got a house, a job, a man—"

"I thought I told you to stay away from that Greek boy, Anna."

"Well, Mom, you also told me that Dad cheated on you, but we all know that's not true."

"Oh, shit," Lizzy whispered, and the line was quiet for a long moment.

"Anna Theresa Linton, my relationship with that man was very complicated. You will never be able to understand just how complicated."

"I understand more than you know," Anna said, looking over to the letters on the coffee table.

"Well, whatever you think you know, it doesn't change the fact that Linton women have never done well on that island."

"You mean *you* have never done *good* on the island. All *you* did was cause heartache and destruction. And I don't want to do the same thing as you."

"How dare you pretend to know what I went through," Grace said, in a voice louder than Anna had heard from her mother in a long time. "I think this conversation is over. Goodbye."

The line clicked, and Lizzy started to laugh.

"Damn, Banana. That was intense."

Anna laughed as well. "Yeah, probably a bit uncalled for."

"No, I'd say it was a long time coming. But, Banana?"

"Yeah, Liz?"

"I think it's great if you want to stay. But just be careful you're not doing it because of Mom."

Anna frowned. "I wouldn't decide where to live just

because of how far it is from her. Though I can't pretend that's not a plus."

"That's not what I meant." Lizzy paused. "You're so desperate not to turn into her, not to do what she did. And I get that. She's always been a bitch, and it sounds like it was no different when she was there. But if you're going to stay, make sure it's not just the opposite of what she did. Make sure it's what you actually want."

Grace,

I had a heart attack yesterday. Not a big one. The doctors didn't have to operate; they just gave me aspirin and kept me overnight. But still, I thought you would want to know.

My parents are predictably devastated. My dad has told me I'm not allowed to work anymore. A neighborhood boy I have grown close to over the years is taking over my shifts until I'm back on my feet. Not that you care about any of that but, frankly, this hospital room is boring and I have nothing better to do than write to you.

This kid is great, Grace. He reminds me a lot of Lizzy, actually. He loves helping other people, but he doesn't want anyone to notice. He's smart, but he doesn't care about that stuff. I actually made him go to college so he would have options, but sure enough he came back the second I hit the floor. He could do anything he wants in the world, but all he wants is to live here and work for my dad. Weird kid. But, then again, you've got one of them, too. Of course, him being so similar to Lizzy means they'd never get along. Actually, I bet he and Anna would like each other, if she's anything like I imagine she is. Who knows?

They say that when you have a near-death experience, your life flashes before your eyes. Well, my heart attack must not have been serious enough, because that didn't happen to me. It hurt like hell, but apparently not enough.

But what I did have was a moment of clarity. My biggest regret isn't leaving. I think it was the only way forward. We had passed the point of no return a long time before that. No, my biggest regret is not accepting the way things actually were between us. If I had been honest with myself, then we could have been happy. Not necessarily together, but we at least could have dropped the charade and figured something out. Something that would have meant I could be with my children and you could have a life closer to the one you imagined. Green Card marriages happen all the time between people who don't love each other but care enough about each other to work out an arrangement. If I could have put aside my broken heart and my pride, maybe we could have had something similar.

But that's not what happened, and I can't change

anything. All I can do is hope that I live long enough to see my girls someday. I've long stopped hoping that opportunity would come from you. All I can hope is that something brings them to me so that we can finally know each other.

I'm going to give you the benefit of the doubt that you've raised happy, healthy girls and say THANK YOU. If they can't have their father, at least they have their mother. Hopefully you're happier now than you were when we were together. I really do wish you the best.

Yours,
Giorgos

A nna pulled up to the Summerhouse on her new Vespa, parking it in her new driveway under her new trellis covered in pink flowers. She took her helmet off and wiped the sweat from it with her tee shirt. She took off her backpack, too, trying to ignore how it felt almost stuck to her back as she did. If she had thought it was hot when she first arrived on the island, she was eating those words now. It was the first time she had driven herself back from work instead of walking or being driven in the truck, and it was absolutely glorious to not have to trudge up the hill or wait around for Christos or Nikos to pick her, but it was no less sweltering under that helmet. She walked through the gate and turned the corner toward the front door.

"You're late," Elena said, and Anna saw that she was sat on the edge of the patio. "I've been here for a full hour." She didn't look hugely distressed, a Greek magazine in her hands and a glass of something – probably from Eirini – next to her, the condensation forming a ring on the white cement. She smiled up at Anna as she approached.

"I know, I'm sorry," Anna said, unlocking the door and motioning for Elena to come through. "My shift ran late because of some tourists who wouldn't leave, and then I had to go get gas."

"For your new motorbike?"

Anna nodded.

"Seems a bit useless if you're leaving soon," Elena muttered under her breath, and Anna pretended not to hear her.

As she came inside, she hung her helmet on the new hook by the door and put her shoes in the basket underneath. Elena followed suit. Anna switched on the air conditioning unit she had bought for the window and stood in front of it as the air began to blow, slowly cooling as it did.

"That's okay," Elena said. "I started calling them anyway."

"Oh, yeah?" Anna began unpacking her backpack on the table, pulling out a table runner, a pack of fairy lights, and two towels with a pretty filigree design stitched into them. Elena had promised to call some local estate agents for her and speak to them about the property. Anna had tried to do it herself, but their English was almost as bad as her Greek. So instead, she emailed before and after photos and a copy of the previous valuation, and Elena was following up on the phone. "What did they say?"

"They all said the same thing," she said. "That the market is doing well right now, the economy is recovering, and the pictures you sent through indicate that you may have doubled or even tripled the value of the house."

"That's great," Anna said, though she didn't smile. She took the towels into the bathroom, removed the tags and started hanging them on the new handrail.

"Is it?" Elena asked, following Anna into the bathroom. "I still don't understand what's going on here, Anna."

"I'm not sure what's confusing about it," she said. "I fixed up the house, and now I plan to put it on the market."

"Yeah, but why?" Elena asked, sitting down on the lid of the toilet. "Aren't you happy here?"

Anna stopped adjusting the towels and looked at Elena, exasperated. "Of course, I am."

"And don't you love the house?"

"You know I do," she said. "But it's not that simple."

"Yeah, yeah, that's what you keep saying."

"And I mean it," Anna said. "I'm happy right now, but I don't know if I can be happy here long-term."

"And why is that?"

Anna sat down on the edge of the tub. "I feel like I'm repeating myself over and over again," she said. "I feel like this is the millionth time I've had this conversation."

"Yeah, well, me too," Elena replied quietly, sighing. "But you keep making no sense."

Anna had almost told Elena and Nikos about winning the contest at least a dozen times. But every time she wanted to she became afraid of their reaction. She didn't want to seem like one of those frigid bitches from Hallmark movies who always chose their careers over everything else. They're not the heroines, they're the girl at the beginning of the film that breaks the heart of the romantic lead. And even though that's very probably what Anna would be doing, she didn't want to feel that way.

"If I've learned anything from my dad's letters, it's that pretending everything is working doesn't do people any favors."

"Yes, but that's ancient history," Elena said, throwing her hands up. "You are not your parents."

Anna shook her head. "No, I'm not. And I'm not going to repeat their mistakes. I'm going to cut my losses before anyone gets hurt."

"No," Elena said, shaking her head as well. "I'm not accepting that anymore. You know you're hurting us anyway when you say you can't be happy here, right?"

"Nikos said the same thing."

"I'm not surprised. He's probably more hurt than anyone."

"That's not my goal," Anna said. "But I do honestly think it will hurt less this way."

Elena stood up. "Whatever, Anna. Let's just finish these calls."

Every other time Anna and Elena had had this argument, they'd been able to go back to friends immediately after. But for the rest of the afternoon, Elena was distant. Even cold at times. Anna figured she probably felt like the end was near. And Anna wasn't certain she could tell her it wasn't.

Meanwhile, Anna couldn't keep her mind off the fact that Nikos was meant to be out with Vasilis's sister Maria tonight. The last she'd heard, they were meant to be eating dinner at the pizza place down the road from the resort. She felt a pang of jealousy as she imagined someone else sat across from him on a date.

"I hope Nikos is having a great time," she said to Elena as she pulled their dinner out of the oven a couple of hours later, "but I'm also worried about what it means for us hanging out. Do you think he'd stop coming around?"

"So what if he did? You're the one who's leaving."

"I mean, I'm not gone yet," she said, and Elena laughed.

"Wow," she said. "You think you're really something, don't you?"

Anna froze. "What do you mean?"

"I mean that you're allowed to cut your losses by leaving on your terms, but we're not allowed to cut our losses before then? What gives you the right to decide that for us?"

Anna shook her head. She was getting really tired of having arguments in this kitchen. "I didn't mean it that way."

"No, I know what you meant," Elena said, standing up from the table. "I am, believe it or not, emotionally intelligent enough to understand what's happening here, even if you're not."

Anna took off her oven mitts and threw them down on the counter. "I think I understand my own situation perfectly well, thank you very much."

"Not as far as I can see." Elena crossed her arms.

"Okay then, why don't you tell me how it is," Anna said, crossing her arms as well and leaning against the kitchen counter, trying to act casual despite the fact that she could feel her face going red.

"Let's see... Well, for starters, you weren't happy back home." Elena started pacing the floor. "You were in a shitty non-relationship with your boss at a job that you didn't actually like but didn't feel like you could leave. And when you found out about the house, you jumped at the chance to shake things up a bit by coming out here. But when the option to go back to your crap life in New York was taken away from you, you convinced yourself that getting back there would prove everyone wrong. Then you actually started to fall in love with this place, but your pride is keeping you from admitting it and doing what would probably be the right thing for you. But I don't really care about the right thing for *you* anymore. Not the way I care about the right thing for my family. And the right thing for us is to not be around someone who constantly hurts us."

Anna could feel the tears forming, but she fought them back. She wasn't going to give Elena the satisfaction of being right. Plus, if she defended herself, there's no way she could avoid mentioning the gallery placement. And with Elena bringing up Marcus like that, there was no way she was going to do that.

But Elena was right, wasn't she? The second Anna had been fired, she had started to romanticize her life back home, even as she built one in Greece. She had it way better here than she'd ever had it in Manhattan. Or Connecticut for that matter, at least since Lizzy left home at eighteen. Or maybe even since her dad left.

Now she was being given a chance at that life in Manhattan. Marcus finally wanted her, and she didn't want to waste that opportunity. So why did she keep buying things like she was sticking around? Elena was right that she wasn't being consistent. She had one foot in each possibility, and it was splitting her in two. She had been feeling that tension the entire time she had been there. She just hadn't realized that it was splitting her friends apart as well.

Anna started to cry, unable to hold the tears back any longer. Elena softened a bit, and for a moment Anna thought that she was going to come comfort her. But she seemed to catch herself, re-crossing her arms, her jaw set.

"You're absolutely right," Anna said. "I don't want to hurt you guys. You're the best friends I've had in a long time."

This time, Elena did step forward, but she still didn't

reach out for Anna. "You're a good friend, too," she said. "But you've got to make up your mind what you're going to do, or you're not going to have options anywhere."

Anna nodded. "I know. I will."

Elena reached out and put a hand on Anna's shoulder. Then someone knocked on the door, and a couple of seconds later it opened, and Nikos walked inside.

Anna couldn't stop her heart from surging at the sight of him. She knew he was probably on his way to meet Maria, but that didn't stop her from being glad to see him.

"What's going on?" he said, seeing Anna crying and rushing over. He wrapped her in a hug, and the tears started to come harder and heavier. She leaned into his chest, feeling the wetness spread on his shirt, damp against her cheek.

"Anna's just having a little crisis," Elena said from behind him, her exasperation with the situation clear from her tone.

"Well, we're here for you," Nikos said. Anna looked up to see Elena rolling her eyes.

"That's okay," Anna said. "I think I have to figure this one out alone. But thank you." She pulled back from Nikos.

"Well, I have some good news that might cheer you up," he said. "Grab your phone and check your email. There should be one from Xenia."

Anna walked over to the table and picked up her phone,

opening up her emails. The top one was from Marcus, just a series of question marks. She had gotten nearly a dozen of these over the last week, begging her to accept the prize. She flicked that one away to archive it. The next one was from Xenia, with the subject line "FWD: European Commercial Photography Awards." She tapped on the email to read it, nearly dropped the phone as she did.

Dear Xenia,

We wanted to contact you about the photography featured in your recent marketing campaign for the Kamari Sands Resort. The photography was discovered and nominated by a member of our committee. It was a last-minute addition to the ballot, but we are pleased to inform you that the photos have been selected as the winning campaign for the "Hospitality Photography" category and shortlisted for the overall European Commercial Photography Award. The €10.000 prize for this category is to be split equally between you and your photographer, so if you would be so kind as to send through his or her details as well as your own, we would love to arrange the payment.

Also, for being shortlisted for the €100.000 grand prize, you are to be invited to London for the award ceremony next month on Friday the 6th of September. Your hotel will be provided for the night of the ceremony, along with dinner and breakfast. Once we have your photographer's contact information, we can send through the event details.

We look forward to your reply.

Kind regards,
James Bennett, Chair, European Commercial Photography Awards

"What is it?" Elena asked, craning her neck to try to read over Anna's shoulder.

"I won an award," she whispered. "For the pictures of the resort."

"That's amazing," she said, and she actually smiled. "Well done, Anna. Those photos were incredible. You deserve it."

"Tell her about the grand prize," Nikos said, raising his eyebrows.

"What grand prize?"

"It seems I won for the hospitality category," Anna said, "but I've also been shortlisted for the European Commercial Photography Awards overall category."

Elena was definitely smiling now. Maybe things weren't so irreparable between them after all. "That really is amazing," she said, wrapping her arms around Anna for a moment. "Congratulations."

"Thank you," she said, but she could barely get the words out with everything that was going through her mind. Her cheeks were still damp and her throat sore from crying and fighting with Elena. She needed to get some air. She needed to be alone.

Anna looked up at Nikos. "Did you come just for this?" she asked. "You should probably be on your way to meet Maria."

Nikos shook his head. "I cancelled that," he said, not making eye contact. Anna felt herself relax just a bit. "I actually came to get Elena."

"What? Why?" Elena asked. "Is everything okay?"

"Yeah, fine," he said. "But when I talked to Xenia, she seemed pretty desperate for someone else to work the bar, and you weren't answering your phone."

"I've been a bit busy," she said, catching Anna's eye. "But, yeah, I'll go."

"Sounds good," he said. "It looks great in here, by the way, Anna. You've made a really lovely home of this old place."

Anna laughed softly. "Thanks," she said. "Too bad I'm always working, and you two are the only ones who get to appreciate it."

"Well, then, you should have a party," he said. "Have everyone from work and town over. Christen the place."

"Isn't that what you do with boats?"

"Meh, we'll crack open a bottle of champagne on the patio," he said with a wink. "It'll be just as exciting, though admittedly less breezy."

"Sure," Anna said after a moment. "I think that sounds like a great idea. I should have everything done by this weekend."

"Great, I'll spread the word!" He started to walk out the door.

"Hope you're able to wrap everything up before then," Elena said, holding Anna's gaze as she gathered her things off the table. Then she followed Nikos out the door and pulled it closed behind her.

Anna knew what she was saying. She was giving her an ultimatum. Anna needed to figure her shit out by the weekend, or Elena was out. And probably Nikos with her.

Anna sat down on her new sofa and leaned against her new throw pillows. She really did love this place. It had started out as wanting a creative outlet, and then it was about carrying out her dad's vision, bonding with him as she did. But somewhere along the way it had started to be for her and only her. Every detail was chosen and curated carefully. She loved every inch of the home she had created. She had put so much money into it, and even more time. She had fallen in love in this house, both with the island and the people who lived on it. When she thought about going back to a cramped studio apartment or house share in New York, she felt terrible. Between her friends and her house and her photography business, she had everything she could need here. She didn't want to leave.

And yet, she couldn't shake the feeling that she should follow her father's advice and cut ties. If she wasn't one hundred per cent sure she could stay forever, then it was probably better for her to get out now. She may not have all of this back in New York, but she did have the possibility of the career she had always dreamed of, that she had wished for every day she sat behind a desk in the gallery staring up at photos she knew were no better than hers.

She wished, not for the first time and probably not the last, that she could talk to her dad about everything. So she did the next best thing and picked up another of his letters. This one was thicker than the others, and as she opened it she saw why.

It was actually two letters, and, instead of being to her mother like all the others, they were for her and Lizzy.

Anna glanced briefly at Lizzy's, curious about what it might say, but she quickly decided to put it aside and save it for her sister. She took the two pages meant for her and went into the bathroom, where she could see the sky changing color through the window. She sat down in the tub, as she'd taken to doing, and began to read.

My dearest Anna,
I've started letters to you every single year for the last nineteen, but this is the first time I've been brave enough to finish one and send it.

I don't know what your mother's told you about me. I don't know what you think of me. But one important thing is true: I love you. I always have. And I never betrayed you.

If your mother has actually told you anything, you

might have known that five years ago I had a heart attack. Well, I've actually had a few more since then. Eight, actually. They've all been pretty small, but they worry the doctors. I never let it worry me – it's their job to worry, after all – but I had a pretty scary check-in today, and I knew that I had to write to you.

Today is your twenty-fifth birthday. I can't believe that you are a real, bonafide adult now. Every day I imagine what you look like, what you sound like, what you do... I'm not hoping for any certain thing. I just hope you're happy. That's all I've ever wanted for you and your sister.

I have written plenty of letters to your mother, begging her to let me see you, and they have all come back unopened. I have no reason to think this will make it to you either. But after all these years, not knowing how many I have left, I know I can't sit on what I have to say. I have to try.

I can't imagine what you think of me. If you believe what your mother has undoubtedly said, you probably hate me, and that's fair. I guess that would be the worst-case scenario. But even in the best-case scenario, I'm a stranger. While you always have a home in Greece should you want it, even if just for a few days, I'm not writing you to beg you to come see me. I've done enough of that in my lifetime. No, I just wanted to tell you that I know you're incredible and strong and passionate, and I am so proud of you.

258

You always were so smart and so creative. Wherever you are in life, whatever you are doing, I know you'll be doing what you love. I know you're happy. I just know it. It is the greatest sadness of my life to not know you as you are now, but it is the greatest joy of my life that you are out there somewhere making me proud.

I love you so much, Anna. It's hard to know what to say after all these years to make you believe that, but I trust that if you ever get to read this letter, you'll believe it. I have always loved you, and whatever happens after this life, I'll be loving you then, too.

Love,

Your father

In the middle of the island of Santorini is a village called *Exo Gonia*, the hills of which hide a bright yellow summer house that looks like it's straight out of a story book. The quaint cottage was built by a man full of hopes and dreams for his future, but love and fate were unkind to him. When he died, the summer house was left in disrepair, broken and run-down. Hope had abandoned it long ago

Until, one summer, the man's daughter came to the island and found a home within the summer house. She mended it with her own hands, taking her father's vision and bringing it to life in its walls and windows. And as she built and repaired and created, the hope and passion he had lost began to fill her as well. She chose each detail with great care, filling the home with love and laughter and good food. Her plan had been to create this oasis for another, but as she settled into her father's footsteps and built upon his foundations, she began to wonder if it couldn't be her home, after all.

20

A knock on the door shook Anna out of her reverie as she stared out the bathroom window over the island she had fallen in love with these last few weeks. She dried her hands and walked to the door, opening it to Nikos, who was standing on the stoop with a large, flat present.

"Well, hello," Anna said. "You should come around like this more often."

Nikos laughed. "Just a little housewarming gift, now that the place is done."

"Do you want to come in?"

Nikos pointed over his shoulder. "It's so nice outside. Should we just sit outside for a bit?"

Anna nodded and pulled the door shut behind her. They walked over to the porch swing that had been installed the day before.

"The patio looks amazing," he said, raising his hand to the trellis running over them as they sat. "I can't believe you did all of this in the last three days."

Anna had been very busy indeed. The porch swing

had been easy compared to the trellis, which had been a walk in the park compared to the flat pack desk she had ordered. But now everything was finished, every little detail put together. She had wrapped things up, as Elena had said.

Elena seemed to be giving her the benefit of the doubt that she would make a decision by tomorrow, offering to help with the last-minute party preparations. But Anna had wanted to finish the other things herself.

"Yeah, it took me all night last night to get it finished. But now I just need to decide what to do with the wall over the desk." She looked through the window at the blank white space.

"About that," Nikos said, handing over the gift. "Maybe this will help. It's from Elena and me."

Anna unwrapped the present carefully, excited but not wanting to seem like a child on Christmas morning. When she peeled back the paper, she saw her own face staring back at her. And not just hers, but her father's as well. Tears welled up in her eyes.

"Nikos, this is incredible."

"Kostas's girlfriend did it," he said. "She takes commissions for people, so we sent her a picture of you, and she painted your dad from memory. We thought it was about time you had a picture together, even if it is just a watercolor."

Tears fell on the protective glass as Anna looked at the painting. Her dad looked so much older than she remembered him, which made sense. She had missed nearly twenty years. But yet, somehow, he seemed just right, too. Finally, she had a picture of him.

"We weren't sure for a while if it was a good idea, based on how you felt about him when you arrived, but we thought maybe things had changed."

"They have," she said quietly. "Everything has changed."

For a short moment, Anna and Nikos sat silently on the swing, rocking back and forth, just enjoying each other's company. The last few weeks had been hard on both of them, but they had come out the other side. They were alright. Anna knew that whether they would stay alright probably depended on what she chose to do, but she had decided to embrace just a little bit of hope. She scooted a bit to the left, closing the gap between them, and lay her head on his shoulder.

First, she felt him stiffen for a moment, caught off guard by the advance. Then he relaxed, moving his arm to the back of the swing so her head came to rest on his chest. A few moments later, she felt him gently kiss the top of her head. They stayed like that, cuddling on the swing, until the sun set.

They headed inside, and Nikos cracked open two beers from the fridge, handing one to Anna. The simple domesticity of the evening made her smile. Something had changed when she had read her father's letter to her. She saw Marcus's offer for what it truly was: an excuse. It was the easy way out to go with what she had always thought was right for her – status, clout, recognition. It was much harder to admit that she had been wrong.

Now she knew what she wanted to do. What she *needed* to do. She just hoped Nikos still felt the same way.

"What's all that food in there?" Nikos said, gesturing toward the very full refrigerator.

"Eirini brought it," Anna replied, her voice shaking a bit. "She's making a ton of food for the party tomorrow. I think that's about half of it. I have to cook it all in the morning."

"I can't believe there's more to come. If she brings this much food again tomorrow, I feel like we could feed the island until—"

"You were right," Anna interrupted. As Nikos looked up at her, she felt her face go red and her breathing go shallow.

"I usually am," he said, taking a couple of tentative steps toward her. "About what exactly this time?" He was trying to play it cool, but she could tell from the way his brow kept knitting together that he knew exactly what she was saying.

"Everything," she said, smiling, and she felt like she was going to start crying. "About my dad. About this place. How I feel about it. How I feel about..." she trailed off, gulping as she started to tear up.

He stepped closer still. "About what?"

Her response came out in a whisper. "About you."

He was standing in front of her now, toe to toe, both

her feet firmly in this future. This opportunity. He put a hand on her waist as he lowered his forehead to hers. "Are you sure?" he asked, and she could feel how shaky his break was.

"No," she said honestly, the tears starting to fall. "At least not about anything else. I never have been. I could fail at my dreams just as spectacularly here as I did back home. But I am…" He met her gaze as she paused, and she felt certain of what she wanted, not just in that moment but every moment after. "Nikos, I—"

"I love you," he blurted out, and immediately his eyes went wide, as if he'd shocked himself. She laughed softly.

"I love you, too."

Almost before she could even get the words out, his mouth closed around hers, and he was kissing her. He was kissing her, and he was pressing against her, and he was pressing her against the kitchen cabinets. She reached behind herself and put a hand on the counter, jumping up so that her face was even with his. She wrapped her legs around his waist as his hands grabbed at her back, at her sides, at her clothes, fistfuls of hair and fabric and flesh.

He lifted her up and carried her to the bed, and she wrapped around him as tightly as if her life depended on it. And she felt like it did. Like everything had been hinging on this, and as they came unhinged together everything else was falling into place. Her hips rose to meet him as they kissed, his hunger for her evident in more ways than one. She sat up as he peeled off first her shirt and then his. She pressed up against the skin she had been admiring all this time, feeling his warmth seep into her. He kissed down her neck and her belly, unbuttoning her shorts as he reached them. He brought himself back up to her face and kissed her lips gently.

"Are you sure?" he asked again, and this time she knew there was no turning back. But she was done going back. There was only forward. Only him. Only her. Only now.

"I'm not sure about anything but this," she said, kissing him back. And as he made his way back down her body past the point of no return, she sunk her head into the mattress and smiled.

21

"This is where they write 'and they lived happily ever after' in the sky," Nikos said, tracing her belly button with his finger. He bent down to kiss it, making Anna laugh. He took that as an opening and began tickling her, and they devolved into a fit of laughter until they were so tangled in the sheets they couldn't move. Anna reached her head up to kiss Nikos on the chin.

"Not happily ever after," she said, sitting up and grabbing her shirt. "Not yet. Gotta live our lives first."

Nikos sat up behind her, kissing her on the shoulder. "But happy right now?"

"Happier than I've ever been." She looked him in the eye as she said it so that he would know she meant it.

Just then, the door busted open. "Good morning!" Elena shouted as she walked in, not clocking them as she kicked the door shut and carried a pastry box and a tray of coffees across the room to the table. She put them down and picked up one coffee, turning toward Anna and Nikos. "We've got a lot to do, so get up and get dressed before Ni—"

Elena gasped and almost dropped the coffee when she saw them, spinning away so she wasn't looking at them. Anna and Nikos were grasping for sheets trying to stay covered, and Anna grabbed for her shorts and started putting them on.

"Anna, I think we need to talk outside," she said, stomping out the door.

"Elena, wait just a second," she said, chasing her out the door. "I can explain."

"Explain *what?*" Elena shouted, circling back on Anna and pointing at her. "That you couldn't keep it in your pants?"

Anna stayed calm and composed. In every other discussion, she had gotten defensive. Raised her voice. Sounded desperate. But now that she knew what she wanted and had done what was right for her, she didn't feel the need to argue about it.

"No, that's you," she said with a chuckle. "I've managed to keep it in my pants for seven weeks with a guy I actually love."

"Hey, that's not fair. I'm perfectly capable..." Elena went quiet as she realized what Anna had said. They certainly weren't laughing now. "You love him?"

Anna nodded. "I do."

"So what does that mean?"

She shrugged. "It means that I love him, that's all. And that he loves me."

"And the house?"

"I don't know. But I can't pretend any longer like Nikos isn't a factor. And I can't imagine anything that would make me want to leave the love I've found here."

And in that moment, she meant it. Not Marcus, not the contest – nothing could change her mind.

"Okay," Elena said, nodding along. "I'm happy for you two that you figured that out."

Anna stepped up to Elena and took her hands in her own. "I mean you, too, Elena. I love both of you."

Elena smiled. "You do?"

"I do. I love Eirini and Christos. I love this island. I love this house. I love the food, for Christ's sake. I love my life here. And I don't take that lightly."

Elena leaned in and hugged Anna. "I love you, too," she said. "I just wish things were more certain."

"But are they ever?" she asked, and Elena shrugged. "I'm as certain as I've been about anything. It would take something major to come between us."

"More major than you sleeping with my cousin?"

"I hope so," Anna said with a laugh, "because that ship has sailed. More than once."

Elena landed a playful slap on Anna's arm. "Gross, I don't need to know that."

"Okay, well how about the oven times for the *spanako-pita*? Will that take your mind off it? Because Eirini was very adamant about the specifics."

"Show me the pie," Elena said, throwing her arm around Anna and walking back into the summerhouse.

The three of them worked all morning to get the food ready and the summer house clean. But by one in the afternoon, when Eirini and Christos arrived with the rest of the food, it was pretty much ready to go. Nikos was hanging the painting over the desk just as Eirini walked in.

"Oh, Giorgos," she said, walking over and touching the painting gently. Then she turned to Anna. "He would be so proud of you, you know."

"I hope so," Anna whispered, and she meant it. She wished with all her heart that her father was somewhere looking down on her, seeing what she had done with his house and his legacy and feeling proud of his Anna.

Nikos grabbed Anna's hand, and she squeezed it, leaning into him just a bit. She wasn't ready for huge public displays of affection, but she was glad to have him there and not have to stop herself from reaching out for him.

Eirini looked as though she was going to get emotional, but instead she walked away and started arranging the plates and napkins on the table. The others moved to help her and a few minutes later the guests started arriving.

*   *   *

An hour later, there were over two dozen people shoved inside the house. Anna had hoped to use the patio, but of course it had started raining as soon as she made plans that required outdoor space. Not to mention, Eirini's food was somehow almost gone, so Christos had had to run out for more from the shop down the road.

"So," Xenia said, "have you thought about the awards ceremony in London?"

"Yeah, I think it would be really fun."

"Oh, good." Xenia let out a sigh. "Because I've always wanted to go, but I am *not* a solo traveler."

Anna laughed. "Well, I'm happy to be your adventure buddy."

The door opened slightly, and Anna saw a few shopping bags peek through the opening. She ran to help open the door, and Christos stepped in, both arms full of shopping bags, dripping wet.

"Anna!" he said. "I find friend!"

"What do you mean?" Anna said, but he didn't have to answer. As he came through the door, there was another person coming in behind him.

"Hello, Anna. I believe I'm 'friend.'"

Anna's mouth went dry, and she felt her hands begin to shake. Of all the people to show up at her party, he was the last one she wanted to see.

"Marcus, what the hell are you doing here?"

"Oh, wow," he said. "Not happy to see me?"

271

"Not really," she said, trying not to draw attention to them. "How did you even know I was here?"

"That other award you've won? It was announced online. I came as soon as I saw where you had been hiding out," he said. "I'm here to find out why the hell you aren't responding to my emails about the greatest opportunity you could possibly get to launch your career — an opportunity you accepted."

Anna scoffed. "The greatest opportunity? You really do think you're God's gift, don't you?"

Marcus sighed. "Listen, Anna. I'm not here to get you back. I'm here because you didn't just win that contest. You obliterated the competition. And you deserve the prize far more than anyone else I know."

Anna softened a bit. Hearing those words from Marcus was all she had dreamed of nearly the entire year they were together, and now it was happening. But she had made her decision.

"It's not that simple, Marcus. I can't just go back to New York. I have a life here now."

"Doing what?" he asked. "Taking pictures of hotels for a living? You could have so much more, and you know it."

Anna felt a hand on her back. "Who's this?" Nikos asked, stepping up next to her. He didn't drop his left hand from her back but stuck out his right hand to Marcus. "Nikolas Doukas. Nice to meet you."

Marcus took Nikos's hand for just a second before dropping it. "Yeah, yeah, Marcus MacMillan, nice to meet you.

Could you give us a minute, Romeo? We're having an important conversation."

Elena came up on Anna's other side. "What's going on?"

"Oh, nothing to concern yourself with, sweetheart," Marcus said.

Anna felt Nikos's arm slip from her back as he formed a fist down at his side. She slipped her hand over his and looked around. People were starting to pay attention to their conversation.

"Can we just step outside for a moment?" she said, and though both men protested going outside in the rain, she pushed them through the door. Elena followed, positioning herself between the two men. The rain steamed as it hit the ground, soaking them through almost instantly.

"*Maláka!* Who the fuck is this guy?" Nikos said, muttering what Anna assumed were Greek profanities under his breath.

"This is Marcus," Anna said. "We worked together in New York."

Elena whipped her head around to Anna. "Wait, is this your old boss?"

"Guilty," Marcus said. "Though maybe let's say 'previous' instead of 'old'?"

Nikos looked from Anna to Marcus and back again. "The boss you were sleeping with?"

Anna's stomach dropped. This was getting out of control.

"For over a year," Marcus said. "But don't worry, she

dumped me just before she came here. We haven't touched each other for almost two months."

Anna saw a vein in Nikos's forehead appear that she had never seen before. "You were sleeping with him *days* before you came here?"

Anna shrugged. "Yeah, I was. That's completely irrelevant. The point was that Marcus was here to offer me something, and I declined."

"Wait, *what*? Why? You can't decline, you accepted over a month ago!"

"Offer you what?" Nikos said, speaking over Marcus.

Anna looked first at Nikos. "I'll explain," she said. "Just let me get rid of him." Then she turned to Marcus and took a deep breath. "Because I don't need you, Marcus. I have a life here. People I love. People who want to pay me for my work. And the last thing I need is something getting in the way of that."

Marcus pressed his lips together. "You're making a big mistake. This could be the turning point in your career."

"Then I'll deal with the consequences."

He nodded, backing up toward the gate. "If you change your mind, I'll be at the airport tonight. Ten past nine to Athens. There will be a ticket waiting."

"I won't use it," she called after him as he walked away.

"I hope you do," he said. "I know we have our history but put that aside for a moment. This is too important to walk away from." Then he turned and left through the gate.

Nikos took a step back to face Anna. "You wanna tell me what the hell that was all about?"

The rain lightened up, and they stepped under the trellis, where they were almost fully sheltered. Elena touched Nikos's arm, catching his gaze, then nodded and went back inside.

"Marcus and I are over," Anna said. "He was here for a work thing, nothing else. But I said, no, so it's fine." She put her arms on his torso, trying to wrap them around him, but he was rigid.

"What was he offering you?"

"Nothing important," she said, but as she looked up at him, she could tell he wasn't going to let this go until he had answers. She sighed. "I won a contest at the gallery. The Emerging Talent Contest. He wanted me to come back and show at the gallery for a month. But I said, no."

Nikos closed his eyes and let out a deep breath. "Why would you do that?"

"Because..." she said. "I decided to stay. I told you that. That's why we... why last night happened."

"But why didn't you tell me?"

"Because it didn't matter."

"Can't you see that it does matter?" He put his hands on his head and took a step back. "Of course it matters. This whole time we've been telling you to stay because you didn't have anything back home. But you've been keeping this from us." He looked down at the ground. "How long have you known?"

Anna sighed. "Just over a month."

Nikos snapped his head up. "*A whole month?*" He paced back and forth for a moment, and Anna imagined he was going over the last three weeks in his mind. He paused at the edge of the trellis, looking out over the hills. "So when you told me you wanted to be a real photographer, this is what you meant?"

Anna's lip began to quiver. "Yes, but I don't believe that now," she said. "I love my life here. I love you. None of that was a lie. And this doesn't change anything." She reached out for Nikos, but he stepped away, out into the rain.

"Of course, it does," he said. "It changes everything. How could it not?"

"It doesn't have to," she said, hot tears mingling with cold rain on her face.

"But maybe it should." He crossed his arms and looked her in the eye. "Tell me this wouldn't kick-start your career better than anything else."

Anna tried to do it, to tell him that it wasn't a big deal, but they both knew that would be a lie. It was the opportunity of a lifetime.

Tears formed in Nikos's eyes as well, and he wiped them away, but they kept coming. "You've worked so hard to avoid being like your mother, but the truth is you've always had bigger dreams than this island can hold. Than one man can give you. And I refuse to be the reason you don't get what you want."

Anna stepped toward him again, and he held his hands up this time.

"Nikos, please don't do this," she cried. "I chose you. I love you."

He shook his head, taking another step back. "I decline your choice." And then he turned around and ran through the gate.

Anna collapsed to her knees and began to sob. Huge wails came from her mouth as she slumped against the side of the house, her nose running as she cradled her head in her hands. After a moment, she felt Elena's arms wrap around her, pulling her to her feet and guiding her to the front of the house. At some point, the rain had stopped, and when they got inside, Anna saw that everyone had gone. But the cries didn't stop. She slipped off her shoes and peeled off her clothes, climbing into bed in her wet underwear. She crawled under the duvet, put her head down on the pillow and sobbed some more. She sobbed for Nikos. She sobbed for her father. She sobbed for everyone else she felt slipping away from her as she accepted what had happened. She cried until she fell asleep.

She couldn't have been asleep for long, because it was still bright outside. In fact, it was sunny. The clouds had completely cleared out. She heard a noise from the kitchen, so she looked up to see Elena washing dishes from the party.

"How long have I been asleep?" she asked, her voice more of a croak.

Elena put down the plate she was washing, dried her hands and came over to sit on the edge of the bed. "Just a couple of hours," she said. "It's about six."

Anna sat up and took a drink from the water bottle on her bedside table. "I'm sorry about all of that," she said. "I didn't see that coming."

"I don't think anyone did," Elena replied. "That was kind of the point."

Anna shook her head. She felt like she might cry again, but there were no tears left it seemed. Her eyes just burned hot instead. "I don't understand what happened. After almost two months of telling me I should stay, he tells me to go right when I tell him I want to be with him."

Elena crawled into the bed next to Anna and rubbed her back. "I know it's hard to understand, but you have to remember that Nikos has been hurt before. All those other girls dismissed him for their lives back home, which was hard, but it was fair. But the only thing worse than that would be for you to do the opposite and give up your life for him, only for you to resent him later on. Remember, he saw the after-effects of what happened with your parents. You're not the only one scarred by that particular failure."

"I guess I get that. But it's not like I gave up a rich, full life for him. It was one contest."

"One contest that could lead to the rich, full life you've always pictured," she said. "Which, you have to admit, is very different from the life you have here."

278

"But that doesn't make it *better* than my life here. Just different."

Elena shrugged. "I don't think that makes a huge difference to him right now. He feels like he'd be holding you back, and I don't know how you convince him that that wouldn't be the case."

Anna sat there silently for a while, thinking about what to do. Elena got up to finish the dishes, and Anna went into the bathroom with her phone. She sat down in what had become her spot, the tub, and called the only person she could think to talk to.

"Anna?" Grace answered, sounding surprised. "What's wrong?"

"How do you know something's wrong?" she said, fighting back tears.

"Well, you've been in Greece for almost two months, and you're calling me out of the blue. Call it a lucky guess."

Anna broke down, telling her mother everything that had happened. She expected interjections about how foolish she was being, but she didn't get any. Grace simply listened.

"Well, I think it sounds like you need to come home," she said after Anna was done.

"You don't think I should stay and fight for him?"

Grace sighed. "Anna, something I learned a long time was this: when a man tells you what he wants, believe him. He told you he doesn't want to be with you. It doesn't matter why he said it. He meant it. And you have to respect it." Anna wanted to protest, but she knew her mother was right. Nikos had always been sincere. She knew he hadn't made the decision to end things lightly.

"But what about everything else?" Anna asked. "What about my friends? My job? My house?"

"Your friends, if they're really your friends, will be happy for you," she said. "The house is still your house, unless you decide to sell it. And honestly, sweetie, the job sounds pretty disposable. Ditch the cafe. You've got enough other things going on at the moment."

"I guess you're right," Anna said. And just like that, her entire plan had done a one-eighty in a matter of hours. "I guess I'm coming home then."

After she hung up with her mother, Anna came out of the bathroom to find Elena sitting at the table.

"So, what did Lizzy have to say?" she asked.

"Actually, that wasn't Lizzy. That was my mother."

"You called your *mother*?" Elena said, her eyes wide. "You must be really desperate."

"Yeah, well, this desperate girl is leaving with Marcus," she said, and Elena nodded.

"I saw that coming," she said.

"I didn't."

"I know." Elena hugged her. "Do you want me to help you pack?"

Anna looked around at the summer house; at everything she had installed and bought and created and chosen over the past seven weeks. "You know what?" she said. "I'm only going to take what I brought with me. So I'm okay. But I would love for you to do one thing for me."

Elena hugged her friend tightly, resting her head on Anna's shoulder. "Anything."

"Thank you," Anna said. "I need you to deliver a letter."

Then she opened her computer and began to type.

The taxi pulled up to the airport exactly an hour before her flight was due to take off. The driver took her bags out of the trunk and carried them up to the door for her, and she handed him all of the cash in her wallet as a tip. He looked at her, surprised, and then quickly thanked her and got back in his car, probably afraid she would change her mind. It was certainly better service than she had received from the person who had picked her up at the airport seven weeks earlier, though less impactful, she imagined.

She approached the check-in desk and smiled at the woman working. "I think someone has left a ticket for me?" she asked. "My name's Anna Linton."

"Yes, Mister MacMillan paid for your ticket just a few minutes ago. Let me get that printed for you. Could I have your passport, please?"

"Sure, but just one request. Could you make sure my seat is as far from Mister MacMillan's as possible?"

The agent gave Anna a knowing smile and nodded. "I think I can arrange that."

As the woman checked Anna in and weighed her baggage,

Anna watched the outside for the sign of anyone she knew, but no one was coming for her. She had isolated herself the moment she decided to go back with Marcus. She accepted her boarding pass and passport from the check-in agent, thanked her and headed for security. The lines were short and the security agents friendly, and once she was through, she followed the signs to her departure gate.

When Anna approached the gate, she saw Marcus smiling at her.

"Came to your senses, did you?" he said, standing up as she approached.

Anna took a deep breath and looked him in the eye. "I would like to formally accept your offer to display my collection at MarMac as the winner of the 2018 Photographer to Watch competition. But I have a few details I want to discuss."

"That's fine," Marcus said. "You're making the right decision. We can figure everything else out on the way home." He stuck out his hand. Anna shook it, then picked up her bag and walked across to the other side of the waiting area to sit until boarding started.

Just then, the gate agent's voice came over the loudspeaker. "Attention passengers of Flight Three-Six-One to Athens, I regret to inform you that, due to a staff shortage, your flight has been cancelled."

Nikos paced the floor in his house, trying to decide what to do. No, scratch that. He knew what he wanted to do. He couldn't let her go without at least asking her to stay.

He knew that her flight was at 9:10 p.m., about forty-five minutes from now. It would take less than twenty minutes to get there on the Vespa. He also knew that he had just enough money in his bank account to buy a ticket in order to get past security.

But he couldn't decide what to do with that information.

What do I have to lose? he thought. *Oh, wait, just your dignity when you ask her to stay and she goes with him anyway. She's already proven that she cares more about showing her photos at some fancy gallery than she does about you. Who are you kidding?*

Of course, Nikos knew he was being ridiculous. He knew she had been exercising all the self-control she had to keep him at arm's length for the past few weeks, even when he continually tested the limits of that control. And he had known what he was getting himself into last night. Plus, he had been the one to tell her to go.

Nikos flipped back and forth between the impulse to run after Anna and his resolve to stand his ground. Deep down, he was most afraid of the possibility that she wasn't ever actually that conflicted. That she never really intended to stay. That while he had been falling in love with her, she had been having a good time, just like her mother did before her. Nikos knew that wasn't fair. He wasn't Giorgos, and Anna wasn't Grace. But the story felt painfully familiar, and he didn't want to make the same mistake his dear friend had made in going after a woman who didn't love him back.

But that was it, wasn't it? He loved her. He knew he did. And if he really loved her, there was nothing else he could do.

Nikos grabbed his phone, his passport and his keys and hopped on his Vespa. He knew her plane would start boarding at any minute, so he needed to get there as quickly as possible. He pushed forward into the hills as the sun set around him and willed his little motorbike to move him more quickly toward his destination.

He got to the airport in record time, parking his Vespa and running inside, only to see from the departure boards that the 9:10 flight had been cancelled. Elena called him for the fifth time since he had left the house, but he declined the call as he approached the ticket desk and asked the woman what was going on with the flight.

"The flight to Athens has been cancelled due to a staff shortage," she said in a chipper tone.

"So all of those passengers are stuck here for the night?" he asked, hope building in his chest.

"Actually, those that were continuing on to North America and the UK were rerouted through London on the eight-fifty-five flight. But everyone else has been grounded, yes."

"That's fine," he said, looking at his watch. It was 8:30 p.m., which meant he had made it just in time. "One ticket to London, please." He cringed at how much he was about to spend, but he knew that he needed to speak to her before she left. Before she went back with *him*. Before it was too late. He puffed up his chest and held out his passport.

"Oh, I'm sorry, sir, that plane has already left the gate."

"*What?*" he shouted, his chest deflating instantly. "But it's still almost half an hour to take-off!"

"Well, the flight was full with all the new passengers, and they got an earlier slot, so they taxied out early."

Nikos nodded at the desk attendant, thanked her and walked over to the window. Sure enough, as he pressed his face against the glass, he saw an EasyJet plane ascending into the clouds.

It didn't matter how certain he was that he loved her. He was too late.

Anna had forfeited her right to an airport chase scene the moment she had chosen to live in the real world instead of a rom-com; the moment she had decided that fulfilling her dreams was just as important as the guy she had known for weeks, no matter how much she loved him. Plus, if he had already read her letter, he wouldn't be coming to stop her.

But that didn't make it hurt any less to watch her life in Santorini disappear beneath her as she boarded the plane and found her seat and they took off and flew straight into the sunset.

There was no turning back now.

Nikos,

I am so sorry to have to be writing you this letter instead of telling you in person, but I want to respect your wishes.

After weeks of uncertainty – years, if I'm being honest – I have never felt so secure in my decisions than I did when I woke up next to you this morning. Even if it had to end like this, I'm so glad we had those hours together. They were the best of my life. I wouldn't have changed a thing about them, even to make things happen sooner. I'm glad I waited until I was sure.

You were right about one thing. I definitely would have wondered "what if" if I hadn't taken the placement with Marcus. It would have probably bugged me not knowing what would have happened with it.

But you were wrong, too. My dreams aren't bigger than the island, or bigger than you. Because my dreams are only as big as I am. What matters is how deeply those dreams have rooted themselves in me. And while my dreams of being a critically acclaimed photographer have been there for longer, they haven't reached as deep as my love for you. For the life I built – the life you helped me build – on Santorini. And those roots don't get pulled out as easily as you telling me to leave. The plant may be gone, but the roots remain.

The mistake you and I made was thinking that it

was the falling in love that mattered. That we had to keep falling in love or we would end up like my parents. And with so many other dreams in my heart, it was hard for both of us to imagine that being possible. But look at Eirini and Christos. They've been together for over sixty years, and they're still madly in love. They haven't been falling in love that whole time. They hit the bottom a long time ago. It's the roots that formed and entwined together that keep them happy and in love. It's like the rice throwing at the wedding, willing the bride and groom to become one root. And that root existing underneath it all is more important than anything happening above ground.

You rooted into my heart quickly and thoroughly. I fell in love with you quickly, and I've stayed in love with you. Pretending that root hadn't formed didn't make it any less present. I hope you feel it too. Because I'm not done with you just yet.

Love,

Anna

Epilogue

Two weeks later, Manhattan

Anna paced the floor of the kitchen at the gallery, her second glass of champagne in her hands. The room had filled with prestigious guests, from critics to collectors to other photographers, and any minute now Marcus would introduce her and unveil her collection to them. They would either love it or hate it; there was rarely any in-between with this crowd. And Anna needed them to love it. She needed them to think her work was important. All of her heartache, all of Nikos's heartache, would be for nothing if they didn't love it.

Anna had hoped to hear from Nikos after the letter she had written him, but she hadn't. Not one peep from him or Elena. Or Christos or Eirini. Only Xenia had messaged, asking if she would still be going to London. She knew she didn't deserve a second chance, but she had hoped she would get one anyway. Like her mother, she had run away back to America when something better came along. Unlike her father, though, Nikos was smart enough to let her go. She had told herself she should be happy about that, but selfishly she wished she could have her cake and eat it, too.

"Anna, they need you outside," an assistant said, poking her head through the door. "There's someone trying to get in that's not on the list."

"It's just my mother," she said. "I didn't think she'd be here, so I didn't put her name down."

The assistant shrugged. "You'll have to go tell them that," she said. "I have to do something for Marcus."

Anna rolled her eyes and snuck out the back door. She didn't want to walk through the room full of those deciding her fate until she had to. She walked around the corner of the building, looking for her mother's blonde hair amongst those congregated near the door, but she couldn't see it anywhere. Just as she was about to go back inside, a man turned around, and Anna saw a familiar face looking back at her.

She nearly dropped her phone on the pavement.

"Nikos!" she shouted, rushing toward him. "What the hell are you doing here?"

Nikos smiled and held out his arms, catching Anna in a hug as she lunged at him. She stood on her tiptoes to wrap her arms around his shoulders, burying her face in his hair.

"I couldn't stay away," he said. "I wanted to be here to support you."

Anna leaned back to look at him. He was wearing the suit he had worn to the wedding back on Santorini. "You look so handsome," she said.

"Yeah, well, I was wearing this suit the night I first kissed you. It was one of the best nights of my life. I thought I'd bring it out again for luck."

"You don't need luck, Nikos." Anna felt tears form in her eyes. She brushed them away, not wanting to ruin her makeup before the event, but she couldn't quite catch them all. "And, as I recall, you were wearing a lot less when we actually kissed."

"Yeah, well, Elena told me that showing up in my pants to a black tie event probably wouldn't go down very well."

Anna smiled. "I wouldn't have minded."

"Don't worry," Nikos said with a wink. "I've got them on, too."

They both laughed.

"You could have called, you know," Anna said, wrapping her arms around his neck, craning her neck up toward him.

"Nah, too predictable," he said, pulling her close, whispering in her ear. "You deserve a grand romantic gesture."

"If you recall, things didn't go so well for the last Greek man who followed a Linton woman back to America."

Nikos frowned and shook his head. "You were right. We're not your parents."

"No, we most certainly are *not*," Anna replied, but before she could press her lips to his, she heard a throat clear. She looked over to see Marcus at the door, glaring at her.

"You can have your romantic moment in a bit," he said. "But for now, it's time to introduce you to the world. You ready?"

Anna looked at Nikos, took his hand in hers and nodded to Marcus. "I am now."

"Great. Then get your ass in here."

They followed Marcus inside, and Anna joined him on the temporary stage. Nikos stayed just off to the side where Anna could see him. Then Marcus introduced Anna, and the room erupted in applause as she stepped up to the microphone.

"This is such a huge honor," she said. "Thank you so much to everyone who came." She looked down at the notes she had prepared, then over at Nikos, who smiled at her. She took a deep breath and continued.

"In my opinion, the reason photography is such a powerful medium is because it imbues the subject with importance. Take any ordinary object or any person off the street and photograph them, and you've created an automatic value that wasn't there before. I take very seriously the responsibility to photograph things in a way that tells the whole truth. I entered this contest with a series about forgotten Manhattan landmarks, because the story of New York City so often features the same things over and over.

"But that series is not the one that you will be seeing today."

Anna glanced at Nikos, who was still smiling, but his brow was slightly furrowed.

"This summer, I have fallen in love with the Greek island of Santorini. My father grew up there, and I had the privilege of experiencing the island not as a tourist but as a local. And as many photographs as there are of the sunsets and the beaches and the turquoise waters of the Aegean, and as worthy of photographing as those things are, those aren't the things I fell in love with.

"The island captured my heart, and it did so not through panoramas and party beaches but through the kindness and openness of the people. The homes are built around hospitality. The residents go out of their way to make people feel welcome and accepted. And the most vibrant thing on Santorini isn't the sunset but the souls who inhabit it.

"This isn't the most commercial collection, but I hope that it will invoke a feeling of home and comfort for you. Because when I think of Santorini, I think of home. Thank you."

The room applauded as Anna's photos were revealed all at once. Suddenly, the room was swimming in a sea of color, the blues and yellows and pinks filling the space with force.

Anna pulled Nikos up onto the stage so he could see all the photos. There was one of Eirini stretching filo pastry, one of Elena and Vasilis snuggled up on a public bus, and one of Christos and the guys playing cards on their break at the resort. There was one of a winemaker, one of a shopkeeper, and one of a stable full of donkeys in Oia ready to carry tourists through the winding streets. But Anna's favorite was the one of Nikos from their lunch in Oia, him looking out toward the water with a beer in his hand and a smile on his face.

"Anna, these are incredible," he said. "But did you mean what you said? About Santorini being home?"

"Of course I did," she said. "I already bought a plane ticket back. I leave at the end of next week."

"But what about the rest of the show?"

"That was one of my conditions for Marcus. I would come back and show if he would let me change the collection to new photos and only stick around for the first week. After that, I don't need to be here. The gallery will do everything it can to make money, and if that's from my work, then great. If not, at least I'll be home."

Nikos grinned and picked Anna up, twirling her around before setting her back down. "I love you, Anna."

"I love you too, Nikos. Thank you for coming here."

"There's nowhere I'd rather be."

Then Nikos grabbed Anna's face with both hands and kissed her. And as they kissed, surrounded by images of Santorini and the incredible people who made it feel like home, for the first time, Anna wasn't worried about the future. She had everything that she needed all around her. She had everything she wanted right there in her arms.

Acknowledgements

Having worked in publishing and earned an MA in Creative Writing before ever writing a book, I had heard every cliche about the process: that "feeling inspired" isn't a prerequisite for writing, that effectively self-editing is nigh on impossible, and that structural edits are the actual worst. Having now finished my first novel, I can say with confidence that all of those things are true. However, it is also one of the most fulfilling things I have ever done.

This process would have been genuinely impossible without the incredible team at HarperCollins UK and One More Chapter. To Charlotte Ledger, thanks for letting Santa take a crack at writing a book. To Emily Ruston, your edits are maddeningly brilliant, and working with you has made me a better writer. To Claire Fenby, thank you for being a social media badass. To the talented design team, they say to never judge a book by its cover, but in this case it would be an honour. Thank you so much for a beautiful cover that perfectly conveys what the book is on the inside. To the production team and the pricing team and the rights team and every other team that works so hard to make sure these books make it into the world and into the hands of the right readers, THANK YOU. You are all superheroes to me.

I want to particularly acknowledge my late grandmother Velma Hobbs, née Parks. The character of Eirini featured much more in earlier versions of this novel, and it was her relationship with Anna that inspired me to use my grandmother's maiden name in my pen name. Grandma Hobbs, as I called her, was the most loving, patient, kind, compassionate woman I have ever known, maybe tied with her daughter. I hope to one day be half the woman she was.

For putting up with Sam the Writer (who is far moodier and short-tempered than normal Sam), thank you to my gorgeous husband Alex. You have taught me so much about what love looks and feels like, and I couldn't have written a romance without having lived ours.

Thank you to my mother Lisa Gale, both for reading the first drafts and for having so many friends. You're probably responsible for at least half the sales of my book. Your support means the world to me, and this accomplishment wouldn't be nearly as sweet without you to share it with me.

To Victoria Stevens, one of the most talented writers I know and my dear friend, thank you for inspiring me to do what I love, for paving the way, and for taking me to France where I wrote the first words of this novel.

To Jaye Rockett, thank you for being the most incredible

champion and supporter I could ever ask for. Everyone should be lucky enough to have a friend like you.

To Shermia Roberts, thanks for the kick in the ass when I was avoiding and procrastinating. This book wouldn't exist without you.

And to Evelyn Maniaki, thank you for your help with all things Greek.

Lastly, I want to thank all of you readers who have made it to the end of our journey with Anna. It has been such a privilege to write for you. I hope that life brings you happiness, and that you are able to experience love every single day. I can't wait to share more stories with all of you. Thank you for the opportunity.